1st published in Great Britain 2014
ISBN: 978-0-9926196-6-4

Published by:
The Wacky Wordshop.
40 Emmerson Way
Hadleigh,
Sufolk
IP7 6DJ

http://thewackywordshop.co.uk

Printed and bound by: Amazon CreateSpace

Acknowledgements

Thank you to all my friends for helping me in different situations, especially to Blanche Brown, for drawing a beautiful cover for Timeless. To my family, particularly my Dad, for inspiring me and my Mum, for home-schooling me, a huge big thank you. A special thank you to John, for always making me laugh, to Joseph, for being a lovely brother and to Sarah for being the best sister anyone in the world could wish for!

And finally, a huge thank you to my publisher, Brice Higgins, for helping my biggest dream to finally come true.

Ann's Story

As the cart jolted along a new feeling came over me; one I hadn't experienced before. One can only have so much bad luck; I prayed mine had run out. Fate had not been kind to me; much having already been taken from me. My parents and five siblings all lay in the cold hard earth with not even a cross to mark their place. A bittersweet sadness held my heart and I clung tightly to my sole remaining treasure; my last sister, my only sister, not yet nine years old, innocent and pure as a white rose, more precious to me than gold. Our fortunes hadn't changed but I remained cautiously optimistic about the future. The promise of work had come at a price. Although it was honest work I regretted having had to expose young Bella to the hardships of a scullery maid. But I had no choice. It was this or give her up to death.

The cart's wheels rolled into every pit and over every lump until I was thoroughly bruised and sore. The journey had taken long but with sunset had come a renewed perception of everything around me. Sometimes I'd hear a long shrill whistle that heralded a curly-haired shepherd boy, driving plodding ewes and sprightly lambs down the narrow track, heading home after a long day's work. I rested my cheek against Bella's rough head and allowed a quiet smile to curve my lips. Nothing would go wrong. I held onto that belief.

The first glimpse of my new home filled me with trepidation. Everyone knew about this Hall, the largest for miles around, its acres of land crouching in its black shadow. A heavy iron gate bristled with rusty spikes. From the end of the white stoned drive it glared, like a snooty aristocrat, from its expanse of windows. Gardens laid in straight rows boasted divine smelling flowers and herbs; tall stiff-backed birches hemmed in potatoes and parsnips, carrots and cabbages. It had belonged to the same family for as long as anyone could remember. The current Lord and Lady had expanded it, adding another two floors for their son and daughter. A large forest brooded at the edge of the fields.

My father had worked on one of the farms all year round. When I came of a good working age I was offered a job as well. Not wanting to work further than the nearest field I declined, fearing I wouldn't feel at home in a large, dark, stone house full of cobwebs, dust and a cruel lack of sun and daylight. But as the cold autumn months and icy winter nights crept closer, father died, and then mother. I started to feel panic. Bella's cheek lost their rosiness and my pride wouldn't let me beg, borrow or steal. We slept with aching stomachs. Our bones stuck out sharply. No one needed any field work done in the winter. And I was too proud to go begging for it at the Hall. Only the sight of Bella wasting away quietly, too weak to complain, woke me to reason and made me see sense. I wrote to Fitz Hall, asking for any work they had. Then came the weeks of hopeful, agonizing anticipation, the relief too great for words when affirmation arrived, and the hurried departure from the hovel filled with the dead. I sold everything we had left to buy a cart journey to get here. All I had was Bella. All she had was me. We were all the other had left.

The cart rattled up the drive but then turned sharply left, approaching the side of the house. It looked much the same but in the place of a closed, varnished door there hung a closed, cracked, peeling one. Dusk had set in. Long shadows threw darkness as cold as mountain streams across the neat kitchen garden. I could see robin boxes and bird houses going mouldy in the damp winter air. The cart stopped abruptly, throwing me forward. The driver pointed with a gnarled finger and said, "You're to go in there. That's the servant's entrance." I nodded thanks and understanding and climbed out of the cart, holding out my arms for the sleep-drugged Bella. Together, her tiny shaking hand in my steady one, we walked to the door and I rapped hard. For a long while there came no sound from inside then I heard running feet and stepped back apprehensively. Chains rattled, bolts were slid loudly back and the door opened.

"Yes? It's late. We don't do charity here." The voice, brisk and impatient, belonged to a fierce looking woman. She possessed a pair of spectacles and a set of huge yellow teeth. Feeling rather timid, I spoke up; "We're the new servants," then trailed into silence as she looked us up and down. I knew our faces were dirty and our clothes ragged and torn but I also knew we carried ourselves with straight backs, held there by a pride we refused to lose sight of, and our faces, even Bella's, had not succumbed to the tugs of hunger and cold.

"Oh, yes. Yes, well, you are a bit small," pointing at Bella. "And she is probably also too young." I held Bella's hand tighter and explained, "There was no one to look after her and I could not leave her by herself. She may be small but she is willing to work." The woman looked a bit surprised but nodded grudgingly and stepped back.

"We'll see about that. Come on in then. We don't want all this cold air to get in." She rustled off in a mass of black skirt. I stepped smartly over the threshold and closed the door, sliding back into place the bolts and chains. There was just enough light in the dim passage to see the dark paintings and wooden hooks, cracked with age. We were led up a few flights of stairs all covered with a thin material which looked like it needed changing. Above the musty smell I also detected an aroma of fine food; my nose twitched. We climbed more stairs until I couldn't smell the food and Bella started to lag a bit. Finally we stopped. In front of us were three large doors, all with big brass handles, and the floor was covered with more thin material. The woman opened the final door into a small attic. The roof sloped downwards but there were two beds, both with blankets, a large brass bowl in one corner and a broken chair in the other. Like the outside, it was covered with the same thin material but in places the floor looked up at you, scowling in its filth. The sun poured dusty golden rays through the grimy window. There was another girl, dressed in a long white dress and grey shawl.

"This is Elizabeth, the other scullery maid." said Mrs Langley, the housekeeper, "Elizabeth, this is ..."

"Ann and Bella," I supplied.

"Yes," continued Mrs Langley, distracted. "Elizabeth will fill you in on how we do things here." And she left. We stared at one another across the floor. Elizabeth stood up. She was a good head taller than me, and I wasn't small. Her eyes were the colour of a summer sky and her hair the mirror of gold;

her skin the colour of ripe peaches. I was just black and white next to an explosion of colour; black hair, white skin, black eyes, white limbs. Elizabeth pointed to the bed, "We only expected one person but they can bring in another one if you both want a separate one."

Bella and I moved over to the bed. Elizabeth nodded, smiling faintly. "Call me Lizzie. Elizabeth is so formal."

"Then we're Ann and Bella. Our names can't change."

"Pleasure to meet you." Then she turned to the chest at the foot of her bed, opened it and began rifling through it. I sat down on the bed, unsure of what to do. Lizzie pointed to the chest at the end of my bed; I hadn't noticed.

"Work has finished for today but we start early tomorrow. I always sleep early. You two probably should also." I helped Bella take off her dress and folded it neatly, stowing it away in the chest. She would need a new one. We both needed new ones. Here I could get them. Then I changed myself. Bella and I fell asleep very quickly, wrapped in each other's arms.

§

Lizzie was right; they did give me work, and lots of it. I worked everywhere both in the house and outside. I was the lowest of the low. Cooks, gardeners, butlers and maids could order me about wherever and whenever they wanted. I scrubbed pots in the hot noisy kitchen, dusted pictures, paintings and furniture in the big bedrooms and halls, washed and ironed clothes in the steamy wash-house and scuttled about the whole day long. Every muscle and bone I had ached every night but I felt a small thrill of glee when feasting my tired eyes on the shiny coins I was given. I treasured them carefully, hiding them in the recesses of my clothes chest. These coins meant safety. This money meant freedom and gave me a new start from my old life. Lizzie and I were, from the start, firm friends. She was what anyone would hope for. Bella made sure to endear herself to everyone. Mrs Langley was strict, sometimes too harsh, an unpleasant character, almost indifferent to the suffering of others, as long as the work was done. She was not lazy, but simply expected the rest of the household to have the same energy and determination, however slightly manic, as she had. But Bella had made sure to endear herself to everyone and, in her own childish way, had just as much determination as Mrs Langley and it wasn't long before her innocent face and child-like 'Hello, Mrs Langley' made a smile light up even her bony face. The work was not at all fun; the wash-house a weekly torture. Twelve girls in a steamy room rinsing sheets was almost more than I could bear. The heat didn't warm you; it soaked you in your own sweat and pressed down on you in a thick, humid blanket. My hands blistered and softened, presenting more of a difficulty as the days wore on. My back ached and I dreaded every day. I was good at working in the gardens but hated it. The sun beat down mercilessly and the back of my neck got badly burned. Some gardeners had hats. But we were left to slave in the heat. However there were also things I looked forward to. I loved working by myself in the house; making the beds, righting the furniture and dusting the many books. The library was heaven for me; row upon row upon row of books on every topic and culture and race and plant and tree and bird.

Sometimes I slipped one off the shelf and opened it, but only when I knew no one would come in and then only because my legs wouldn't turn until my eyes had gorged themselves on the forbidden knowledge. Some were in strange texts I couldn't read and some in curly writing I couldn't decipher. But the illustrations were more than enough for me. Martens and unicorns danced between orange fire-eaters and the princesses' mouths opened so realistically I could almost hear their singing bursting from the illustrations. The yellowed pages rustled as I turned them, each one more beautiful than the last. The many rooms were full of curious artefacts; some I couldn't make head or tail of. I was sure I'd become a familiar figure to the inhabitants of the many chambers and halls. There were suits of armour lurking in every corner and shields hung on the walls. One room was full of the stuffed heads of deer, glowering down at me, and the floor was covered in rich oriental rugs and carpets. The day everyone looked forward to was Sunday; hardly surprising as everyone had the morning off. Here we changed our clothes, tied back our hair and attended church, like the pious household we were should. For the first few weeks I sat in the back of the cart, and went along to listen to sermons full of fire and sin and how to repel the shadowy figures of devils with pitchforks; then I gave up. If our point was to listen to God there, I had wasted my time. If He truly existed, He did so in the fresh country air not in the dusty, cold church ridden with mice and the webs of dead spiders. Surely His presence lingered in the sweet scent of wet earth and early morning mist, not in stale incense and burning candle wax. So, when the carts trundled away off the drive, I watched them leave from my attic then slipped downstairs, careful to avoid any stragglers. I didn't want to be caught. I would then run in the opposite direction, toward the sloping fields and conceal myself among the grasses and wheat. Then I would walk, going whichever way my feet carried me, wearing off the week's hard work. The north fields weren't as extensive as the others and rose after about ten minute walk to the rear, in a slope that curved up and then sharply down into a valley. The valley didn't belong to anyone so I felt perfectly at ease there. It was at least five miles across and stretched left and right as far as the eye could see; unbroken, a patchwork of knee-high clover and gorse. At the bottom, a river came from the mountains; on the opposite side lay another forest; dark, dense and deep as well water. I always stayed on the sunny side of the valley, harvesting daises in their hundreds, turning them into necklaces and bracelets for myself. I did invite Lizzie and Bella but they declined and, although I was disappointed for some time, I began to appreciate the unfolding of the book of independence, the one closed to me for so long.

It was on one of these days when a very strange thing happened. I was sitting in the usual place; under the apple tree that offered little protection from the sun. The forest was deserted, as usual, when I distinctly saw someone come galloping out on horseback, and then turn and head back to the forest. I stood up, shading my eyes, but saw nothing. Unsettled, I sat down again, twisting the daisies in my hand. Despite the light material of my dress, I was sweltering rather heavily and my legs and arms had become uncomfortably hot again. I finished my necklace, keeping one eye on the forest, and started on another, plucking the daises from the hard ground. Then I saw them again, much closer this time, almost opposite me on the other side of the river...a rider and horse, galloping across the ground. Laying my daisy chain across my lap I stood up, shading my eyes against the glare of the sun. The air was so still and despite their distance I could hear them well. When they reached the water, both boy and horse drank for some time before starting off again. The ground was steep but the horse climbed it easily. I realised they were headed straight toward me. If they'd seen me they gave no sign, carrying on, their minds totally focused on one another. I waited, watching them come closer and closer. The horse was tall with a high head and glossy mane and tail. The boy sitting high above me, riding the stallion bareback, was a strange-looking one, like a beggar boy...but one from a fairytale.

§

He was a small boy, just skin and bones. But his arms and legs were ridged with muscle. Behind the pleasant twinkling in his eye I could see they were as deep and unpredictable as the unreachable depths of the ocean. His skin was burnt brown and his nails were full of dirt. He wore a pair of cut trousers, all tattered and torn, and a faded yellow and red top so old its threads had come undone. With a friendly smile he asked my name. I told him.

"Hello. I'm Zac."

"Hello," I replied, not sure of what to say and not wanting to appear surly. I squinted up at him, sitting on his horse, as he asked, "You work in the Hall?"

"Yes. I'm a scullery-maid."

"Oh. Is the Master at home?"

"No. He's at church, I think. I've never met him

though. They won't be back for some time. Why?"
He just smiled. He looked about ten or eleven years old, but his posture made him appear older, at least fifteen, and his voice also sounded older. I stared up at him atop his horse.

"When will he be home?"

"I'm not sure. Church takes some time," I responded quickly.

"Will you be heading back soon?"

"Yes."

"Will you see the Master?"

"No."

"Can you see the Master?"

"No."

"Why not?"

"It isn't my place to see him," I said at last.

"You're a good scullery-maid." He was still smiling. Feeling rather ruffled I asked, sharply, "What are you doing here anyway? You could have stolen that horse for all I know. That's a bad crime, you know."

"The first is none of your business. The second I deny. The third I know but I didn't."

"And how do I know to trust you?"

"You don't."

I glared at him. He said nothing. Glancing around, I decided it was my turn to go and stood up. I didn't want to spend any more time with him anyway.

"Where are you going?" he asked, moving his horse to stand in front of me.

"Home."

"Can you take a message for me?"

"Do you mean to the Master? Did you not listen? I told you, I won't see him."

"I know. But someone will, won't they? And you can see someone."

"Well, I'll try." Zac smiled. He didn't just smile with his mouth; he smiled with his entire being until his whole body glowed. He pulled from somewhere in his shirt a package. He leaned down and held it out to me. I took it gingerly and looked at it. It was very heavy and large. I turned it over and saw a deep red stain spreading across the back ... blood? Zac didn't seem worried by it, but it took great self-control for me not to drop it.

"Please give this to the Master."

"Well, I'll try."

"If it doesn't work, then bring it back here next Sunday or whenever you see me."

"But what if I don't see you?"

"You will." He turned his horse and they galloped back down the valley, the horse's hooves throwing up dust, dirt and dry moss. I turned and headed for home. There was something about him; something I didn't want to know and I started wishing I'd never seen him.

It was a pleasant walk back to the house. The evening breeze carried the scent of flowers' perfume and warm bread. The purple of the night spilled across the stark orange of the day like wine over cloth and in the centre of the sky was a small bright light; the last wave of the sun before it disappeared over the horizon. But it was tainted by the steady weight of the package bumping against my legs. Why was it so important? What was in it? As I walked through the fields I became aware of an ache in my legs, like a stitch, but sharper. Blaming my long walk, I pressed on, gritting my teeth. I was lucky with the time. The back door had not yet been locked although I knew I had taken longer than usual.

I met no one on my steady climb to the attic. I was very tired, and short sharp stabs of pain coursed regularly through my legs. I pulled myself into the attic. Bella greeted me by throwing herself at me, asking, "Where have you been? You've been a lot longer than usual."

"Yes, I'm sorry, I know. I didn't realise how late it was and it took me longer to walk back." I looked at Lizzie. My legs really hurt and I wanted to sit down. My friend was looking at me, concerned. "Are you alright? You look hurt."

"No, I'm fine." I winced as another pain shot through my legs. "Actually, I think I need to sit down. Don't worry Bella, I'm fine." She had pulled away as if I had a contagious disease. The pain had become an insistent throbbing as I sat down on my bed. As I started taking off my day dress, I felt something run over my knee and down my shin. Puzzled I lifted the hem of my dress. Lizzie gasped. Running in pretty little patterns down both legs were bright, scarlet trickles of blood. I stood up and probed the skin further up my leg just above my knee and felt a pang of pain. Feeling sick, I looked at the place where the package had touched. A large red welt bled profusely, sending trickles that grew into streams down my leg. The other leg was identical. The room blurred into double vision. I felt woozy, with a strange buzzing in my head and the welt bled increasingly. I saw a red stain seeping onto my dress. I swayed. Lizzie grabbed my arm.

"Ann! What happened?"

I managed to murmur, "I don't know."

The floor rushed up toward me and I heard Bella

shout my name.

When I woke, I was lying in my bed and Bella was peering down at me.

"She's awake!" she crowed triumphantly and proceeded to climb on top of me. I sat up, wincing as I felt my scabs crackle. Lizzie came over, still looking worried.

"Are you all right now? You haven't been out long, just one night."

"Yes. Where is my dress?" and I looked around. Lizzie went over to the wash stand and brought it over. I felt in its pocket. Yes, the package was still there. I took it out and turned it over, looking at the red stain on the back. It was blood. The letter was some kind of parasite. Lizzie opened my chest and took out my other grey dress; the old one bore remnants of blood. I only had two.

"You'd better hurry up and get dressed. If Mrs Langley found out, she'll send you to the town doctor and everyone will make such a fuss. You can have the easy jobs but we must hurry. I just bandaged them for now but ..."

She stopped as I swung my legs over the side of the bed and stood up. They felt like hollow reeds.

"Ann, what happened?" asked Lizzie. By way of explanation, I handed her the package. She took it, looking puzzled and turned it over, her eye catching sight of the stain. Shrieking, she dropped it immediately.

"I know," and I went about the task of getting dressed. The wool, which had seemed so soft, now felt scratchy and painful against the thin bandages.

"I was meant to give them to the Master but now…"

I grimaced. Lizzie had gone to stand at the door,

looking down at the letters in strong disgust.

"It's as if they were alive," she muttered, then came to help me plait Bella's hair. When all three of us were ready, I looked at the letters again.

"What do we do with them? If we gave them to the Master ..?" I trailed away. Scullery maids could be dismissed for the least thing and this was hardly little.

"We'll have to take them with us," decided Lizzie. "Wrap them in something then we'll go and burn them."

With a pang, I remembered my promise to Zac, and then remembered my wounded legs.

"It's hardly fair," I muttered and concentrated on walking without limping. The package spent the day in my pocket, its constant bumping a reminder it was still there. Even the simplest jobs were an arduous task for me. I got through the day by sheer willpower. When I returned to my attic that evening, I changed my bandages then opened my chest. Among the things I had brought to Fitz Hall was a small tinderbox, complete with candle, flint and snippets of wood. My father had given it to me on my fourteenth birthday. I loved it. Pulling back a corner of the thin material covering the floor I took out the candle, lit it, then pulled out the package. Using some of the oil from Lizzie's lamp I dampened the parchment of the package then tipped some of the liquid candle wax onto the letter to help sustain the burning. Lighting it involved burning my fingers and almost setting the floor on fire, but at last I saw the fire lick at one side of the parchment. Crouching beside it, I waited for it to blaze, ready with the wad of sackcloth I had used to wrap it in case the fire got too high. But the flames smouldered out. I blew on the charred paper but nothing happened. It couldn't be burnt. Covering a corner firmly in the sackcloth, I picked it up and looked closer. The parchment was barely damaged. When Lizzie and Bella came in they found me still examining the paper, turning it over and over.

"Ann! What are you doing? Why does it smell of smoke in here?"

I gestured at the letters. "They won't burn. I tried."

Lizzie slowly took in the scene; the charred floor, the still burning candle and finally the letter that was not even scorched.

"I think," she said slowly and carefully, "I think we should open it."

"Why? It's none of our business."

"Because there's something strange in that thing and we'll all get into trouble if we give it to him. We should just open it, see what it is, then go and bury it, in the fields somewhere. I don't like it. There's something not normal about this and we shouldn't mess with it. We should definitely not give it to the Master."

I reluctantly agreed but I made Bella sit on the bed, away from the package. Sitting around the stub of candle Lizzie and I, after several attempts, managed to rip open the parchment and look inside.

There was a locket, about the size and roundness of a chicken egg, pale red in colour. It hung from a golden chain … tarnished slightly around the hook attaching it to the locket ring. There was also another letter. Bumping heads and rubbing shoulders, feeling a little apprehensive, we read the letter …

To the Master
Your work has been done to grave results and this
locket holds the result. It took longer than expected
because the horse went missing before we could
find them and it was hard to bind them. But it has
worked. Before I tell you how we did it, because I am
sure you will want to know, let me warn you about
some things.
The content of this locket is now extremely strong
even though she has been starved for so long. Any
contact with living flesh and she will start to feed, on
whatever she can and for as long as she can. So do
not touch it with bare skin. And also wool and cotton
will have no effect on this because both come from
something living.

We paused, looked at each other and carried on
reading.

You may hold the chain. I must also warn you that it
is not a peaceful spirit; in fact it is very angry and
does not like to be trapped. And the last thing is, DO
NOT TRY THIS EXPERIMENT OUT ON ANOTHER
HUMAN BEING. THE CONSEQUENCES ARE
TOO SEVERE.

I closed my eyes and stopped reading. There was
something alive in that locket; the letter had said so.
What was the Master doing? Who was the Master?
And who was trapped inside? Lizzie finished reading
and stepped away.
"That's sick," she whispered. Bella was looking at
us with a mixture of concern and curiosity. I held out
my arms and she climbed into them.
"Now listen very carefully," I told her, stroking hair

back from her forehead, "That locket is a bad locket and you must not touch it, alright? Don't even pick it up. We have to get rid of it."

"Yes," agreed Lizzie. "And next Sunday we go far away and bury it, do you understand?" Bella's eyes had widened considerably but she nodded. Lizzie covered the locket with the sackcloth and locked it in her chest. Then we changed and got into bed. When Bella's breathing had deepened and her little face changed from serious to satisfied, I pulled the rickety stool up to Lizzie's bed and shook her gently.

"Lizzie! Are you awake?"

"Mmmm… is that locket bothering you?"

"Yes," I admitted, casting a glance at the chest. "But something else is bothering me as well. Has anyone died in this house?" Lizzie sat up then and hugged her blanket around her. She stared at the opposite wall for some time then sighed.

"You might as well know. Yes, a girl has died in this house. It was all covered up quickly because no one knows the exact cause of her death."

"I don't understand."

"She was nineteen and it was her birthday. The Master had given her a beautiful, black stallion. She loved it. But she had a problem with her bones. The doctor had said she would never recover and so never ride but the Master wouldn't believe it, so he gave her this horse. He wanted both his children to be strong and fit. She went out on horseback and never came back."

"What do you mean?"

"Well, the horse never came back and neither did she. When they went out to look for tracks, nothing was found. Of course it was all covered up quickly. She was given a quiet funeral and nothing more was said."

"I see," I murmured, bowing my head. But later, when I was under my blanket ready to go to sleep, I hissed across the room again.

"Lizzie?"

"Yes."

"What was her name? The name of the daughter?"

"Sara. Her name was Sara."

§

It was Sunday, and for the first time I was not the only one who stayed away from church. This time Bella and Lizzie had come with me, bringing a small hand shovel we'd taken from one of the flower beds. The letter and locket were tied very tightly in a sackcloth bag. I had told Bella it would be better if she went to church but she'd cried so much I'd taken her with me; privately, I'd wanted to go to church in case we met Zac. We slipped across the fields heading towards my hidden valley. The ground was mostly uphill and we made slow progress, mostly because of our cumbersome dresses and the heat. My wounds had not yet healed completely but I was faster than Bella and Lizzie, always slightly behind me. When we reached the valley, Lizzie leaned over, hands on knees, panting heavily. I smiled.

"Difficult?" I teased. Secretly, I was thrilled that I wasn't out of breath. My weekly walks had strengthened me, mentally and physically, and my more self-centred side was happy; I was beating flawless Elizabeth for once. Taking the trowel from Bella, who had insisted she carry it the whole way, I led the way down toward the river where the ground would be softer and easier to dig. There we sliced and cut the earth until we had a small hole. Over it, Lizzie and I had the same feelings; regret and relief.

We buried the whole bag and covered it with all the excess dirt. Lizzie crossed herself and, after a pause, so did Bella. I didn't believe in all that, so I didn't move. Then Lizzie stamped down hard on the earth, took Bella's hand and they started up the side of the valley. I gazed intently down at the damp mud. I didn't follow.

"Come on, Ann. We'll be missed if we stay much longer," called Lizzie, and I started.

"We won't," I muttered to myself. "I've been here a million times." But I trailed after them anyway.

"Mrs Langley wants you," Lizzie said that evening, looking anxious. "Over there." I groaned and put down my food. I was hungry and wanted to eat and I had to get the extra jobs. Just my luck. Lizzie smiled. "Do you want me to go instead?"

"No," I said. "Don't worry about it." She grinned back at me, swept her hair out of the way and sat down in my place, next to Bella. I allowed my face to curve into a smile as I watched the small brown head rest on the high blond shoulder.

"Mrs Langley?" I asked when I saw her just outside the kitchen.

"Yes, Ann?"

"You asked to see me?"

"Oh, yes. Yes, follow me please."

I followed her towards the stairs with the curious feeling I was being dragged. We didn't have a candle and it was very dark. She stopped suddenly, picked up something off a dark shelf and handed it to me. It was a bundle of old rags.

"Take these upstairs. Third floor. Last corridor. There is a door at the end. Just knock. If you are not answered open the door and just leave them inside. Understand?" I nodded and she bustled off, rather too hurriedly. I mounted the stairs and followed her instructions. The corridor in question was not decorated in the usual style of the house. It was simply whitewashed. The carpet was older than others I had seen. It was not even a servants' corridor; at this the hair on my neck prickled. It was lighter up here, and I saw I wasn't carrying rags, but shreds of torn dresses. I walked to the end of the corridor, my footsteps loud even on the carpet and knocked quietly on the door. There was no answer. I knocked again, louder this time, but again no answer. I looked back down the corridor but there no one in sight. I pressed down on the handle and slowly entered the room.

The first thing I noticed was the candle light, dozens of candles, and wax dripping onto the floor. In the corner was a desk strewn with letters, with an inkwell chained to it. It was a small room artfully decorated with sleek furniture. The candlelight cast black, distorted shadows across the whitewashed walls. I turned round and jumped. Hanging behind me, nailed into the wall, were two sets of manacles, a pair for the ankles and a pair for the wrists. I scuttled backwards, holding the material tightly to me before remembering my instructions. I lowered my bundle onto the floor and was about to leave when I heard a low, questioning voice, "Who's there?" Someone stepped out of the shadows.

He was tall, with a stern and perfectly-angled face. Yet he looked very young, maybe only a couple of years older than me. Was this the Master? He was dressed in the most expensive clothes I had ever seen; all velvet and slashed materials and padding. Lizzie had said he had children. I realised I was staring and took an involuntary step back, quickly curtsying.

"Who are you?" He didn't seem annoyed at all. On the contrary, he seemed politely intrigued at my presence.

"Ann, Sir. I was told to bring you these." I bent down, picked up the bundle of clothes and held them out.

"Oh, yes." He came forward and took them. "Are they from Mrs Langley?" I nodded. He cleared a space on his desk for them and opened them. I couldn't see what was inside because he had blocked my view but he seemed pleased.

"Good, good," he said and turned back to me. "What did you say your name was again?"

"Ann, Sir."

"Are you new?"

"Yes, Sir."

He looked thoughtful. "You have a sister?"

"Yes, Sir."

"And what is her name?"

"Bella, Sir."

"I see. Well, you may go, and thank you for these. They will help me a lot." I started to leave but he called me back. "Oh, and Ann, don't tell anyone where you went, do you understand?" I nodded and stepped back outside. I left for the kitchen immediately.

§

Dinner had finished by the time I arrived back in the kitchen so I took an apple from one of the fruit bowls and some bread and headed upstairs. Bella and Lizzie were already sleeping, Bella curled up next to Lizzie, thumb in her mouth. I smiled fondly down at her then snuggled into my own blankets; they felt surprisingly cold without Bella. I wrapped them around me then took a bite of my bread, chewing thoughtfully. Unbidden, the image of the Master rose in my mind again and I noticed, with a sudden ripple of shock, that it took some effort to push it away. Ever since the locket, I tried not to take things as they seemed. What was in those bundles? And why did he ... if he was the Master ... and the person the locket was intended for, want it? The questions zoomed around my head until I fell asleep.

The next morning, Bella and Lizzie both wanted to know what I'd done the evening before. Evidently the locket was still on Lizzie's mind, but it was just childish fancy on Bella's.

"I just had to do something for Mrs Langley." I brushed Bella's hair back into its customary plait. "Nothing interesting. Just some fetching and carrying work." I winced at the lie. I didn't like telling lies and didn't like how easily this one had come. But I had been told not to tell anyone. I had already not done what Zac had told me, and I broke the rules every week by not going to church.

"Can I come next time?" asked Bella, twisting round to look at me when I'd finished.

"Yes. Next time I will ask whether you can come too. Maybe all three of us will go together," I said smiling, stroking her head. But then I looked at Lizzie and my heart sank; I saw she hadn't believed a word I'd said. I kept my smile plastered to my face as I cheerfully said, "Bella, go down to Mrs Langley. Lizzie and I will be down in a moment." Bella, equally cheerfully, obliged and the door closed behind us. I turned round and immediately started to talk.

"Lizzie, don't ask me. I can't tell you what happened. I was made to promise that I wouldn't." Lizzie blinked. "But I wouldn't tell. I promise. It's about that locket, isn't it?"

"Yes," I admitted. "But I can't. I would tell you if I could, I promise. But I was told not to tell anyone."

"Friends trust each other, Ann."

"I trust you," I shot back.

"You have a funny way of showing it. I won't tell Bella. We don't have to tell anyone else. Maybe I can help you figure it out. You showed the locket to me."

"I know Lizzie, I know. But this was different. Mrs Langley and the Master told me not to say anything." As much as Zac unnerved me, the man I had met yesterday scared me more. I had said I would keep it a secret, and that was what I was going to do. She cocked an eyebrow. "You spoke to the Master?"

"Yes, sort of."

She gave me an angry smile. "You can't have. The Master has gone away on a business trip. He's not expected back for another week. Don't lie to me, Ann. You're no better than me really." I stared after her, open-mouthed.

Lizzie didn't talk to me that whole day although I noticed the hurt looks she kept pointedly shooting in my direction. By the next morning I felt sure she was trying to punish me for lying to her. I had also noticed that Bella treated Lizzie like a sister too, and added to that I felt sure Lizzie was trying to encourage it. Together they chatted as Lizzie brushed out Bella's hair, and, for once, I didn't join in their conversation. I felt sure Lizzie was trying to antagonize me so I refused to rise. I could have my secrets, like she probably had hers. Even if we were best friends, I didn't have to share everything with her. I twisted my hair into a bun and fixed it in place with a pin. Then I smoothed down my dress and left the room, experiencing a small pang of jealously as Bella laughed at something Lizzie said. I collected the pail of coal from the kitchen and began lighting the fires. I found myself telling my hands exactly what to do, determined not to let my mind wander. Sweep the grate. Put in new coal. Light the coal and wood. And the same with the rest of the fires. That day I was put in the wash house. When Mrs Langley told me I stifled a groan and trudged outside. It was a good day outside; sunny and bright with a cool breeze blowing, but that didn't change the fact that in the wash house the smell and heat made it hard to breathe. I stood next to Pippa. Together we dragged the huge sheets in and out of the water and scrubbed at them with the bars of soap. I didn't talk much to Pippa, but we were on speaking terms.

"What's going on with you and Lizzie?" she asked. I pretended I hadn't heard and rubbed vigorously at the sheet and some invisible stain.

"Ann?" This time I couldn't pretend and looked up.

"Yes?" She repeated the question.

"Oh. Nothing. What makes you think that?"

"Only the fact that this morning she came down to breakfast with Bella and you weren't there."

"I had to work." Pippa held her tongue and said no more. I closed my eyes momentarily. I didn't want anything to come between Lizzie and me. Not for the Master. Not for anyone. We were a trio; Bella, Lizzie and I; a group. We couldn't be separated. I lifted the sheet with Pippa and hung it over the line that ran along from one side of the wash house to the other. The bushes outside were full; that's where we usually put them. The door opened. Everyone stopped what they were doing and looked up. Mrs Langley stood there. She came in and inspected what we were doing, reprimanding several girls for not having done it properly. Then, opening the door she pointed to another basket of sheets standing outside. "I want this done as well," she snapped, pushing her way outside again. There was a communal sigh of dismay, from me too, then the sound of scrubbing again. Dusk had settled over the house by the time we were done. I put my hands on my hips, rubbing them, feeling the insistent aching in my back lessen and then disappear. I hadn't been in the wash house very much recently, therefore my aches and pains weren't so bad. I walked with Pippa back to the house. To distract myself, I asked Pippa whether she was done. "Almost. I still have to put out all the fires. What about you?"

"No, I'm done. I had to light them all."

She chuckled. "Well, I prefer my job to yours."

I smiled but didn't answer. She asked another question. "What exactly are you doing here then?"

"I have to provide for Bella," I shrugged and when Pippa didn't answer, I said in defence, "I wasn't going to let her starve. Both my parents are dead."

"Oh. I'm sorry, Ann," said Pippa quietly. I shrugged again. "What about you?"

"Well, my parents work in the village. They're cobblers. I didn't want to be a cobbler so I looked for work here because we couldn't pay the rent." It felt strange to be discussing this as if it were something as trivial as the weather. We walked around the back of the house. Beyond the wall, I knew the fields lay. "Have you ever been to the fields over there?" I asked. Pippa looked and shook her head, shuddering. "No. No, I don't like the countryside. I prefer big houses like this." She looked happily up at the towering brick walls. "And the Master's daughter died out there. Miss Sara, you know." I cricked my neck as I spun my head around. "But, he's so young! He had a daughter?" Pippa looked baffled. "He's very old, Ann." I brought to mind the picture of the Master I knew.

"He can't be much more than twenty though," I murmured more to myself but Pippa heard. She laughed, breaking me out of my reverie.

"Oh! That's the Master's son. His name is Charles. Sara and he didn't get along at all, I heard."

"His son?"

"Yes," and Pippa laughed. "He's almost twenty-five, you know."

"My parents lived into their fifties," I snapped but apologized hastily. "Sorry. I was just thinking." Together we walked into the kitchen where we parted company. I went up to my attic and Pippa went to find Mrs Langley. As I opened the door, I found Bella and Lizzie sitting on Lizzie's bed. Bella was holding some ribbons and Lizzie was plaiting her hair. With their smiling faces and similar coloured hair, they could have been sisters. Bella was so fair and Lizzie's yellow locks complemented it well. I stopped in the doorway, not wanting to disturb them, looking down at my hands instead. Bella looked up as the door creaked and I smiled at her. She didn't jump off the bed, as she would usually have done. She only waved and then addressed Lizzie again, "Go on with the story; what happened then." Lizzie smiled and took another of the ribbons from her hand, weaving it into her hair. "Well, the jealous sister was defeated and the beautiful friend with the even more beautiful princess went to live in the castle."

"And what was in the castle?" prompted Bella. She'd obviously heard this story many times. Lizzie gave a low laugh. "Lots of flowers and gold and silver and many dresses and when the princess wore them, she became even more beautiful. There you are, all done." Bella's hands immediately went up to touch her hair and she laughed. "Oh, thank you. Ann, look what Lizzie has done with my hair."

"It's lovely, Bella," but to my dismay the phrase came out very stiffly and I knew they'd heard. Bella stopped her spinning and came to stand beside me. "What's wrong?"

"Nothing, Bella, nothing." I tried giving her a reassuring smile. She snuggled up as I raised myself on my elbow to blow out the candle. The last thing I saw of Lizzie before blowing it out was her eyes, glinting angrily at me across the room.

§

Lizzie had been right about the Master. He'd gone on a business trip and on his return there was to be a huge banquet. We'd known about it for weeks but still, on the day before, there seemed too much to do. The entire house had to be cleaned, the food prepared, all the gardens tidied and the outside swept. And, of course, that meant Lizzie, Bella and I were running around non-stop. We were had to eat our lunches on the move. I discreetly let Bella sit and rest for a bit but Lizzie wouldn't let me stop for a moment because I wouldn't let her anywhere near Bella. I was sweeping along one of the top corridors,

humming quietly to myself, when I heard the creak
of gentle footfall behind one of the doors nearby
that led to a hall. The picture of the Master's son
rose in my mind again, and I slipped as quietly as I
could into one of the rooms I knew to be deserted.
Putting my ear to the door I heard the handle click
open and the sound of assured steps walking briskly
up the corridor. They paused, carried on then paused
outside my door. I manoeuvred myself against the
wall and bit my lip to stop any fast, loud breaths
escaping. The door opened and I squeezed my eyes
tight shut, shrinking down into the corner.

"Ann?" The voice didn't sound like the Master's son
but I thought I knew it. I must have made a sound
because a head suddenly poked around the door and
I saw the glint of grinning teeth.

"What are you doing, hiding in a broom cupboard?"

"Zac?"

"Yes, it's me."

I gripped my broom firmly by its handle,
straightened my dress and came out of the room. Zac
looked me up and down. He was almost the same
height as me despite looking so young.

"So," he repeated. "What were you doing in there?"

"I thought you were someone else," I said
defensively. "Anyway, what are you doing here? Are
you allowed to be here?"

"No. Well, not really. But I was looking for you. I
have been looking all day. At first I thought you
were avoiding me so I was going to surprise you, but
obviously you heard me." His eyes darted toward
the still open door and I saw a shadow of his former
grin.

"No, I didn't know you were there, actually. Why
did you want to speak to me?"

"I wanted to talk to you about the package I gave you." I felt a block of ice slide down my throat into my stomach where it sat. I lowered my head selfconsciously and started sweeping again.

"Yes, what about it?"

"Where is it?"

"I gave it, like you said I should," and then trailed away because he was smiling and shaking his head again.

"You're a bad liar, Ann," he said, "And I know you didn't. I saw you bury it in the river, and I got it back." He reached into his pocket and took it out. The locket gleamed dully in his hand, evidently unharmed by its recent dunking. I took a step back.

"Zac, that thing is evil. You should have seen what it did to me. I can't give that to anyone."

"You have to," he replied quietly, holding it out to me.

"Why?"

"Because you said you would." All I could do was gape.

"That thing, why isn't it hurting you?"

"I made it. It won't hurt its maker. And it won't hurt you now because you fed it."

"Ugh. No, Zac, I can't. I won't. I refuse."

"Why won't you?"

"Because if it hurts the Master, I'll lose my job and I can't afford that to happen. Plus, it isn't right to give something like that away. You should just destroy it."

Zac withdrew his hand and replaced the locket in his pocket. "I can't. Fine. I'll wait. Or maybe I'll give it myself." He touched my arm. "Bye Ann."

"Bye Zac." He opened the door and disappeared.

I waited each day to see if Zac would turn up again. Whenever I went outside I'd look up at the window of the third floor and wonder what went on up there. Had Charles got what he wanted? Summer passed through and the rich colour of autumn swept across the country. In the house you couldn't see it, but in the woods all the trees shrugged off their green jackets and clad themselves in spindly red woollen cloaks. Conkers swelled and fell and the nuts burst open with ripeness. Soon we'd all be expected to help with the harvest; digging up potatoes from their warm earthy bed and plucking apples and berries. The people from the village were employed cheaply to help with this also. I hoped Zac might come. There was more to him than met the eye and I had many more questions for him. It was cold the day Mrs Langley cornered me again in the kitchen and told me I was wanted once again. I winced when I saw Lizzie standing nearby; she'd clearly heard what had been said. She flashed me a glare but I looked away.

"Yes, Mrs Langley."

"You need to go right away. He was insistent on that."

"Yes, Mrs Langley. Shall I finish the floors first?"

"No, no, Elizabeth shall do that. You just go."

I gave the mop to Lizzie. She snatched it away and stamped off toward the stairs where the water was kept. I sighed. I wanted to be friends with her but this was bigger than either of us; besides, I needed this job. I wouldn't risk my welfare, and Bella's, for the sake of a friendship.

I knocked quietly on his door again and this time I heard a brisk, "Come in." I opened the door. It was almost exactly the same except its windows were open and the candles all blown out. There was also another wooden table facing his, covered with old dresses and skirts and also a small knife. Charles was sitting behind his table, quill in hand, writing something very fast. He didn't look up. I waited a few moments. When he finally did, his face changed in a moment from impatience to surprise.

"Ann, what are you doing here?"

"Mrs Langley said you wanted me."

"Ah. I didn't need you till this afternoon actually, but you might as well start." He gestured toward the other table. Walking across on trembling legs I sat down on the chair. He pushed his chair away from the table and walked around to stand next to me. He laid something down on the table beside me, a long strip of fraying fabric, pale pink in colour.

"I need you to tear up all these dresses to about this size with this," and he reached across me to pick up the knife. "Understand?"

"Yes sir."

"Good. And make sure they are neat. This is very important to me."

"Yes sir." Taking the knife from him I dragged one toward me, surprised at the weight of it. The bodice was completely covered with small pink and white seed pearls; around the neckline were ruffles of white lace. I stood up in order to see better what I was doing. Holding the knife firmly in one hand and pulling the fabric apart to expose the neat line of white stitches beneath, I slit the bodice away from the skirt with a few clean strokes. The skirt itself was made up from many layers of petticoats, and looser underskirts which I ripped away from the main outer skirt which was heavy and embroidered.

Disgusted at having to destroy such a thing I laid the strip on the outer edge of the skirt, cut up it, across and down. Pulling away the stray threads I picked up one strip and laid it next to the pale pink one. Then I continued. Measure, line up, cut. Measure, line up, cut. The bodices I laid to one side with an inward sigh of regret. Just one would allow Bella and me to get out of this place and away to the city. I had heard there were great prospects in the city, great work opportunities. Then I felt a wrench of guilt. And what about Lizzie? What about Zac? Could I just leave all those people behind me? Like I had done with my parents and brothers and sisters?

"That's the third time you've sighed, Ann," came Charles' irritable voice from his desk. "What is the matter?"

I blushed bright red. I hadn't realised I'd been thinking aloud. "I'm sorry, Sir. I was just thinking about things."

He raised both eyebrows. "Well, if you must think, do it quietly."

"Yes, Sir."

By the time I'd finished, my fingers were aching and sore and I hated even the sight of the dresses, let alone the strips.

"Sir, I'm done," I whispered, terrified of making him annoyed again. All through my work, I'd been facing the manacles. They probably weren't there for show, so why were they there? And why did he need all these strips? Charles picked up one of the strips, scrutinized it carefully and then nodded in satisfaction.

"Well done. That will do nicely. You may go now."

"Yes, Sir."

I left the room, nursing my aching fingers. On the

way down the stairs, I met Mrs Langley coming up.
"Oh, you're finished at last."
"Yes."
"Well, you may go and clean in the library as a
treat. I believe Elizabeth is there too." She made
to move on but I asked quickly, knowing full well
I may be punished, "Mrs Langley, please may I do
something else today?" She blinked. Obviously no
one had asked her this before. I dropped my head
and curtsied but didn't move.
"Why?" she asked, fixing me with a beady stare
from behind her massive spectacles.
"I would just like to, please."
"Fair enough. Go and help in the garden. They're
lacking hands there." And she bustled off. However
much I hated the garden, the library with Lizzie
would have been even worse. I shuffled off outside
to help, taking the trowel from the kitchen with me.
I was assigned one of the flower beds to weed and
spent the rest of the afternoon pulling up the tiny
leaves and sprouts that had dared poke their heads
through the soil. When I was done I was muddy
and dirty and everything ached. My dress was also
dirty and the still healing wounds on the inside of
my legs had started to sting again. That was odd;
for some time they hadn't. Maybe it was the work. I
went back to the kitchen, took the wood basket and
ran about the house as the darkness fell, sweeping
the grate and adding wood where necessary. Too
tired to want to eat, I climbed the attic stairs; they
seemed much longer this time, and opened the door.
Lizzie was already there, apparently wanting a
confrontation. She stood up.
"Where's Bella?" I interrupted.
"I left her downstairs eating." I narrowed my eyes at

her. "Did you tell her where you were going?"

"Yes. I care about her too, you know. You're not the only person allowed to do that."

"I was asking because I want to know where she is. She's not old enough to look after herself for long periods of time, and I am her sister. I think I'm allowed to do that."

"You were asking because you think I'm not going to look after her properly. You're not even around her much anymore. Most of my work is done with her while you go off to help Mrs Langley and the so called Master." She spat the words out, clearly angry and hurt. "But she's so young. I want a friend my age, someone I can talk to and I thought we were friends. I thought we were friends like I wanted to be. But why won't you tell me? Why won't you talk to me? Where did you go today? Or have you been promised not to tell?" She watched as I walked toward my bed and sat down, the mattress sinking beneath me. I looked up wearily.

"No, today I think I can tell. I was just cutting up dresses, just making them into strips."

"Why?"

"I don't know."

"For who?"

"The Master's son."

"Was he there?"

"Yes. But he just sat there while I worked. He didn't say anything to me, I promise." Lizzie sank down onto her bed.

"You know, he isn't exactly a safe person to be around." I nodded, lying back on my bed and closing my eyes.

"I know. He has two pairs of manacles nailed to his wall." I heard Lizzie gasp.

"What do you think they're for?"

"I don't know."

"Ann, I'm worried. I think you should stay away." I propped myself up on my elbow.

"I know I should. I get a bad feeling when I'm around him." It felt good to tell someone. Lizzie leaned forward. "So why do you go?" she pressed urgently.

"I don't have a choice really, do I?" I murmured sleepily. Before I slipped into a slumber, I heard Lizzie quietly say, "You always have a choice."

§

The breakfast tables were empty as I arrived next morning, after I'd lit all the fires. Bella and Lizzie, along with the rest of the kitchen staff, were grouped in a huddle, chattering excitedly. I joined them hoping to pick up a few words, and distinctly heard, "... little gypsy boy I heard. He stole Sara's horse. But they've got him now." I tapped Lizzie's shoulder.

"What happened?" She didn't look at me but her voice wasn't hard when she answered, "They caught a little boy on Sara's horse last night. He said he had something for the Master's son and had found the horse, but everyone thinks he's lying of course." Zac. It had to be Zac. Lizzie turned to look at me as I staggered backwards.

"What's the matter Ann?"

"When did it happen?" I asked slowly, my mind whirring. If only I'd taken the locket to Charles when told to! Lizzie took my arm to steady me.

"Last night. One of the gardeners saw it happen. You look awful, Ann, are you really alright?"

"I'm fine. Really. I just need to eat something. But what happened, exactly?" Lizzie sat me down at one of the tables and sank onto a bench opposite. The crowd had slowly begun to disperse but you could hear the story still circulating.

"Well the boy rode through the front gates on horseback. Someone must have been watching from the window or maybe they'd even expected him, because, apparently, the Master's men came out, dragged him from the horse and started beating him, pretty badly." She paused. I leaned forward slightly.

"Yes? And then what happened?"

"Well, apparently the Master's son came out and stopped them, then took the boy away. They put the horse in the stables. It is Sara's, apparently. And so now everyone thinks ..." and she trailed away, suddenly looking all upset.

"That he had something to do with her death?" I finished, dread in my heart. Did he have something to do with her death? Did he have something to do with the locket? And what exactly was in it?

"Lizzie? Where's Mrs Langley? Have you seen her?"

"Yes. She'll be here in a moment."

Mrs Langley seemed to take longer than ever to enter the kitchen that morning. When she did, she first lectured the cooks at length on the state of yesterday's food, and then inspected the cleanliness of the pots and pans, gleaming with water. Finally, after all that, gave out the list of jobs for the day. She dismissed Lizzie, who took Bella with her, then turned to me.

"Go on. You know where to go." I nodded once, behaving with decorum until she couldn't see me anymore, then ran as fast as I could for the third floor. Before knocking I waited outside a few moments, to recover my breath. Then I straightened and raised my hand to knock. I hadn't even touched the wood before the door swung open. The room was exactly as I had left it, except behind Charles' desk sat Zac. The manacles were lying on the desk in front of him. He was cleaning them vigorously with an old rag. A pot of something smelly stood beside him. Every now and then he'd dip the rag into the pot and carry on scrubbing. His long hair had flopped over his face. He raised his head when the door banged against the wall. I gasped. A great purple bruise flowered from the corner of his right eye down to his neck; his left eye was swollen shut. Despite this he gave a small smile when he saw me, then hastily turned and went on scrubbing. I closed the door behind me. Charles sat at the other desk, his table was laden with scrolls and pieces of paper, as before, but he wasn't working; he was watching Zac intently. He looked up as I came in.

"You are not needed today."

"Yes Sir," I replied instinctively, and started to back out of the room. I'd only wanted to come to see where Zac was.

"But I do need to say something to you." I stopped and turned around.

"Yes, Sir."

"Do you like working as a scullery maid?"

Out of the corner of my eye, I saw Zac falter in his scrubbing, but he recovered so quickly I wondered if I had imagined it.

"It's a job, Sir."

He smiled as if sharing a joke with himself. "Of course. But if you could pick any job in the world, even the ones women can't do as of yet, what would it be?"

"I don't know, Sir. I've never given it much

thought."

"Think quickly now then." I stared at him for a moment then thought. The first thing that came into my head was an author, because I loved the books I saw in the library, but then I remembered the beautiful illuminations and said, "Illustrator."

He nodded thoughtfully and then asked, "Of your own books or other people's?"

"My own."

He formed a steeple with his hands and leant on it, looking at me intently.

"What kind of books would you like to write?"

Without thinking I responded, "Fantasy. Like the ones in the library." He smiled as if he'd found what he'd been looking for. "You've read the books in the library?"

I froze, cursing my stupidity. I was trapped and not trusting myself to speak, nodded once; a tiny little nod. He took a deep breath and pushed himself up from his table. Walking behind it so that he stood on the opposite side of the room to me, he said, "And do you like them?"

"Yes, Sir." He had been pacing slowly back and forth but he stopped when I answered and stood with his back to me.

"And if someone gave you one of those books, the most beautiful one as a present, what would you do?"

"I don't know, Sir," I stammered. He turned to me, raising his eyebrow.

"You have never received a present before?"

"I have."

"And how did you feel when you received it?" His voice had taken on an impatient bite.

"I would feel very happy," I said truthfully. He gave

a musing nod. "You may go now."

I nodded and scrambled backwards out of the room. Just before I closed the door, I saw Zac's face lift up and he mouthed at me, "Go to the valley."

I shut the door.

§

That Sunday came too soon. I was wavering between going to church and going to the valley. The conversation two days earlier with the Master's son had unnerved me. I was worried about the consequences of my confession. We were forbidden to touch any of the things in the house unless cleaning them, and only Mrs Langley dusted the books.

"Don't go," urged Lizzie. We weren't arguing anymore for which I was glad, but we weren't yet close friends again. I had tried my best to make up with her but in vain. She was still angry and I, for my part, was still stubborn. She didn't need to know and I had been told not to tell anyway.

"Come to church. You haven't been for ages. What if you get caught?"

"I'm never caught," I murmured quietly. Bella took my hand. "Please come?"

I smiled down at her. "Maybe next time."

"There's no maybe about it," said Lizzie sharply. "It's the rules. You have to come next time or I'll tell Mrs Langley."

"No, you wouldn't."

"I would," she said with conviction. "It isn't fair that you're the only person who doesn't have to go simply because you're the only one who can sneak away."

"Fine." She had a point. I was only able to miss it because I was the only one in the household stupid or brave enough to sneak away. And also true that it wasn't fair to let Bella and Lizzie keep my secret forever.

"I promise I'll come next week," I said, giving Bella a goodbye hug. Lizzie sniffed and took Bella's hand, sweeping off down the stairs. I watched her go. Maybe I didn't want to make up with her after all.

§

Zac was already there, as he'd said he would be. He sat close to the river, staring across the water at the forest on the other side. He didn't move or say anything until I'd sat next to him, then he turned and smiled at me. His eye had opened but his bruise was still there; the colouring on the side of his face was still as vivid.

"It's a lovely day," he said, by way of greeting.

"I hadn't really thought about it," I replied, averting my eyes, picking up a daisy and twisting the stem into a knot. Zac took a deep breath but I cut across him, staring out to the river as well.

"Why are you here, Zac? Really? To give him that locket?"

Zac sucked air through his teeth. "No."

"Then why? Lizzie told me the Master beat you up? And whose horse was that?" He clenched his fists.

"None of your business. Don't poke your nose in places where it doesn't belong!"

"A girl died, Zac. And she was on that horse when she died!"

"I know she died!" he exploded suddenly. "I know how and I know who did it and I know where and everything. Don't patronize me either! I know more about it than you ever will! I know she died! Don't tell me that!"

"So why didn't you come and tell her family? They

thought it was witchcraft! Why won't you tell them? Don't they have the right to know?"

"I can't. I can't go and tell her family. And even if they want to know, it doesn't mean that they have the right or that I'm going to tell them." His face brooded beneath a thunderous look. I stayed quiet even though I was desperate to ask why. He seemed to guess my thoughts and looked at me.

"If you want to ask a question, think of all the possible answers and ask yourself whether or not you are ready to hear them," he said shortly.

"So, you are a gypsy?" We still didn't look at each other. The question surprised him. He gave a short wry laugh. "I wish. No, I'm just part of a motley group of nomads who found a home in the woods. There's nothing grand about us."

"And why does he want that locket so much?"

Zac got to his feet and walked away, silent. Then he came back. Without sitting down he said, "He needs it because inside it are secrets that have been kept secret forever. He wants those secrets."

"Secrets about what?" I asked, looking up, squinting against the sun.

"About ..." he took a deep breath, "about bringing people back from the dead." I burst out laughing. Did he really believe that? Was that all it was? Zac sat down again and gave me a confused look.

"Why are you laughing? There's nothing funny about it."

"Do you really believe that? That's not possible. I don't believe it."

"Well you should because it's true," he shouted. I stopped laughing when I saw his face.

"You shouldn't laugh Ann. My entire family died because of it. You shouldn't laugh." He was breathing heavily through his nose, his nails were digging into his palms. When he spoke, each word was forced out; he choked on some of them.

"My tribe have been obsessed for centuries with trying to bring people back from the dead. If they could, then they'd be the most powerful people on earth. Everyone would respect them. We were driven from our old home because we were not respected enough: maybe that's what started it. I don't know. But it was all based around your soul or spirit and where it went. And it was thought that the minute it left your body it turned bad, but if you could win it over you could put it back into the body and the person would come back to life. At first it was tried with animals. The people in charge of this withheld it from the rest of the tribe; they didn't want anyone to know. But then one day it worked but with a young doe. All her wounds had healed, she was stronger, and she came back. But there was also something wrong with her; she wrecked our camp then bolted off into the forest. And because of that, the secret leaked out. Naturally, people stood up to them, my family included. They were all killed. All of them. But then that wasn't enough and they tried to bring them back as well. Again it didn't work; they came back changed, so, they were all preserved in lockets and boxes, so they couldn't harm anyone. Except my little brother. They kept him imprisoned and very much alive so that I would work for them. I had no choice. So I did. I captured their animals for them and helped them make whatever they needed. I was told to keep everything secret and I did because they had my brother and he was all I had left. Somehow, the Master heard about us. He was very interested in all we were doing and came to strike a deal with us. If we could prove that it worked he'd help us with whatever we wanted. And so they agreed. He said to do it with his sister who was very ill and needing healing; he'd bring her to us in the woods and say it was his birthday present to her. I went out to meet them at the edge of the woods, just there," and he pointed towards the forest, "and there she was on that big, black horse, so excited thinking she'd be healed. But I knew it would go wrong and tried to lead her away. But they were watching. They came and took her to the camp. And of course it didn't work. It wouldn't have worked. So, they trapped her in the locket. But they said I hadn't kept my part of the agreement and ..." He stopped, clenching his teeth. I finished for him, "... they killed your brother."

He gave one nod and started crying.

"I'm so sorry, Zac," I said, knowing it wouldn't help him at all. It didn't. He swiped at his nose and eyes and carried on, "... I was so angry at them. All I wanted was to get rid of them, all of them, so I stole the locket. By rights, it belonged to me because I had made it, really. So, I took her horse and I took her in the locket. I planned on giving it to the Master, hoping he'd come and destroy my tribe, its entire people had done nothing but cause other people pain. The locket is the only thing linking me to my tribe, to my family. If I have the locket, they cannot harm my family any more than they have. But he doesn't just want the locket; he wants the secrets of how to make them as well. He thinks he can do it better, make them perfect. He says if I help him, he'll help me. And he thinks he can do the same with you. He needs help. Lots of it. And he'll get it, anyway he can." The tears stopped flowing and he looked at me. There might have been even a little twinkle in his eye. "If you get any library books anytime soon, remember what you said."

"If he's trying to do that," I exclaimed vehemently. "He doesn't deserve help! I'll never help him!"

Zac sighed. "Weren't you listening? He will have help. And remember Ann, you have a sister and he knows you do." And then he was gone. I sat for a long time afterwards, mulling over everything I had heard.

True to my word, I followed Lizzie and Bella to church that week. Lizzie, who apparently hadn't believed I'd keep my promise, started acting superior and aloof throughout the journey. Bella, oblivious to the slumbering argument between us, had taken both our hands, seemingly delighted with the whole arrangement. I hadn't left the Hall's grounds for a long time and everything seemed new but also familiar. The church was as I remembered it though. Tall, towering roof, ribbed with thin pieces of stone, stained glass windows and dusty pews. I saw the Master, sitting in the front of the church on his raised pew and, with a shudder, I recognized the long brown hair of Charles sitting up straight beside him. As if sensing I was looking at him, I saw him turn so I ducked my head. I was sitting right at the back of the church. There was no way he could see me. The sermon dragged on and on but I tuned out, wondering instead whether Charles was raising the dead for religious purposes or for something else. Did he really want to know about life after death? Was that why he sat so upright, listening so intently? Apparently. I slumped lower on the wooden bench, earning a disapproving look from Lizzie. I ignored it. After church I waited with Bella and Lizzie while everyone loaded themselves onto the carts and coaches. We had to wait for the longest because we were the lowest in the house. Finally, we were dragged up. I had Bella placed firmly on my lap and the cart trundled off, bumping on the potholes. By the time we got back I was feeling rather queasy. After the Sunday lunch came the cleaning of all the plates and cutlery and glasses; up to the elbows in hot water and soap, scrubbing at the china and glass, steam billowing into my face. The kitchen was very noisy with the banging of metal pans, the voices of the cooks shouting orders, the sizzling of the cooking food and the splashing of the water. There was a constant rustling of sweeping dresses and the rapping of shoes on the kitchen floor and the cheerful shouting of people's conversation above everything else. Oven doors slammed shut; heat rippling out from the glowing coals, wine was poured onto one of the dishes, a great hiss issuing from the frying pan. Everywhere there was noise and confusion and activity. Bella was carefully wiping down all the wooden tables while Lizzie was hunched over in the corner, peeling potatoes with a razor sharp knife. I finished cleaning the dishes then joined her, pulling a stool out from under the table. It was late at night when we finally finished. Bella took my hand and leant against my arm, yawning. "Are you very tired?" I asked. She nodded, her head bobbing forward. I left the pail of coal in the kitchen and propped the brush upright next to it. One of the cooks nodded in a friendly way toward us and I nodded back, half carrying, half dragging Bella up the stairs with me. I pushed open the attic door and it creaked in protest, dragging on the ground.

Lizzie wasn't there yet. She would probably still be working. I hummed to myself, going through the customary ritual of brushing Bella's hair and plaiting it, then doing the same with mine, sweeping the comb through my long thick hair. I wasn't pretty but I was proud of my hair, a long lustrous mane of it. Bella was asleep, snoring gently by the time Lizzie entered. I looked up once to notice she was carrying something in her arms and then went back to sorting things in my chest. I didn't look up again until she was standing right in front of me, holding a large package out to me.

"This is for you," she muttered, avoiding my eyes. I stood up slowly.

"For me?"

"Yes." She shoved it at me. It was well wrapped in my layers of brown paper and tied with a length of thick red string. A heavy package, but soft and flexible. Carefully, so as not to disturb Bella, I unpicked the knot and cautiously unwrapped it. Lizzie sat on her bed, not hiding the fact she was watching intently. I had almost removed all of the wrappings before catching a glimpse of what was inside. Feeling sick, I pushed it away. Lizzie immediately stood up.

"What's wrong? What is it?" I shook my head mutely, walking away from it, knowing exactly who it was from and what it meant. Giving me a quizzical look, Lizzie removed the remaining paper and gasped. It was a dress. Deep red in colour, with slashed sleeves, revealing a dark blue underneath and embroidered with tiny seed pearls; it lay there, so innocent and beautiful. Nausea swept through me. Zac's words echoed through my head, 'He knows what he wants. He'll do anything to get it.' I tuned in again to Lizzie's words, staring at the dress as if it would bite.

"Who sent it? There isn't anything here. It's so beautiful, look."

"Don't touch it!" I shouted suddenly. On her bed, Bella stirred and I hurried forward, tripping over my long nightdress. Lizzie looked at me bemused.

"Why not?"

"It's a mistake," I muttered, hastily scrunching the paper around the dress again. "I'll do something about it tomorrow. Let's just sleep now, okay?" I could see Lizzie wanted to ask more questions but I turned away before she could; luckily she dropped it. Throwing the hated garment into the corner of the room I climbed under the sheet next to Bella. I gently brushed the hair from her face; she smiled in her sleep, snuggling closer to me. I didn't want anything to happen to her. I wasn't going to let anything happen to her.

I didn't wait to tell where I was meant to go the next day. After entrusting the still sleeping Bella into Lizzie's able-bodied care, I shoved the dress under my apron and hurried through the waking house. I didn't see anyone, for which I was glad, because the package bulged out weirdly from under my apron and I didn't want anyone to ask questions. I knew my way around the house pretty well by now and before long I stood before his door again. Pulling the dress out from under my apron, I knocked twice, quietly, hoping he might still be sleeping.

"Come in," said the now familiar voice and, swallowing my fear, I stepped through. Although the rest of the house was slowly awakening, he looked like it was the middle of the afternoon. Like before, he sat at his table, quill in hand, poised to write. He looked up as I entered and his face morphed into a face of pleasant surprise.

"Ann. You're here early."

"Yes, Sir. I wanted to return this." I held out the dress. Nothing changed in his expression and his gaze locked into mine. I was unnerved by his smile of polite surprise as if he had genially wanted to give it to me as a gift.

"Why?" he asked at last. "Do you not like it?" The smile wavered slightly and then faded but ghosts of it still hung around his mouth. I stuttered for a reply.

"I think it is too pretty for a scullery maid to be wearing," I stammered. I hadn't thought he'd ask me why. His face quirked into an almost non-existent smile. He stood up. "Wait here," he said, walking around to the door on the other side of the room. He opened it and walked inside. I stood, frozen to the spot, staring at the door. I was shaking. Was this worth it? A loud crash sounded in the other room. I jumped. Moments later, Charles walked back in, Zac in tow, Zac's face was completely better but his expression guarded. His eyes trailed from my face, to the package in my arms, to Charles then back to me. His face fell. Charles stood in front of Zac, hiding him from view, and addressed me.

"Do you like presents?" I started at the sudden change of subject but nodded slowly, adding, "Some presents, Sir."

"Some presents," he repeated. "Is that so?" I nodded. "And tell me, what do you think is the purpose of a present?"

"I don't understand, Sir."

"What is the purpose of a present?"

"To mark a special day for someone, Sir?"

He raised his eyebrows slightly. "Is that all?"

"I think so, Sir."

His eyes scrutinized me and I felt something cold bead my spine. He was sure to see me shaking. Charles started pacing; two steps to the right then two steps to the left. I looked at his shoes rather than his face.

"And what, Ann, do you think that present was for?" He gestured at the package in my arms. I was silent.

"If you don't know the answer, say so."

"I don't know," I whispered. From within his pocket Charles then took out a locket.

"And what is this? Do you know what this is?" I stared at it, then looked at Zac.

"Do you not have an answer?" His voice was quietly mocking. I shook my head and raised my eyes again. Charles gave another quick smile and then, too fast for me to see, spun round and smashed Zac across the face. I screamed, dropping the dress, my hands flew to my mouth in horror. Zac's lip had split open like a berry and blood poured down his chin. He slumped back against the wall, eyes closed. Charles's expression was completely calm, as if he'd done nothing more unusual than closing a door or opening a window.

"What has he told you?" Although the voice was one of perfect composure, I heard the threat boiling and roiling beneath the surface, eager to get out. I shook my head, dazed, numbness spreading through my body. Zac was struggling to sit up, his eyes slightly dazed.

"Nothing?" he pressed, a smile curving his mouth.

"Nothing." I whispered. Charles raised his eyebrows, and ignoring Zac opened the door they'd just entered through and beckoned to me.

"Come here. I want to show you something." My feet moved involuntarily. I tried to avert my eyes from Zac as I passed him but didn't miss his warning look. The room next down was much smaller, having a faint smell of gunpowder or smoke. The ground was covered in rough carvings; deep gashes were hewn out of the floor. There was no furniture except a small table in the middle of the room. On the table stood a machine, the likes of which I'd never seen before. It was oblong, with a handle on one side. Crouched over the top of it was a candle-stick holder, a stub of wax wedged into it. A piece of polished glass, attached to a spring was positioned over the candle.

"Do you know what this is?" he asked, pointing and looking at it himself with a look of intense pride. "No, Sir." He didn't reply. He simply stared at me. The door to the other room was still ajar and I could see Zac's figure still slumped on the floor, not moving. He held up the locket and showed me it. "What did he tell you about this?" The warning was clear in his voice. I swallowed, and replied as truthfully as I could, "Nothing, Sir." His hand descended out of nowhere and caught me across the face, sending me backwards.

"Don't lie!" he shouted. "He has already told me what he told you. You know what he has come from, and what I am trying to do now." My cheek burned with pain. Humiliated, I felt tears well up in the back of my eyes. He advanced on me, the locket still swinging from his hand. In the dim light, it seemed to glint, mocking me.

"You have a sister, don't you?" he demanded. When I didn't reply he shouted again, "Answer me!" and so I nodded. "Yes, Sir."

"If you tell anyone what I know, that you know about the tribes living in the woods or anything else, it is she who will suffer, do you understand?" The words fell on deaf ears but I nodded mutely.

"Good. Now get out," and he turned his back on me. I left the room shaking. Zac was standing now and when I came out, he looked at me.

"What did he want?"

I bowed my head. Zac sighed.

"You agreed to help him, didn't you?" I couldn't bear the resignation in his voice.

"I'm sorry Zac," I whispered. "He was threatening Bella. I can't lose Bella." His eyes flashed.

"But still? For that price?"

"For Bella, anything." Zac's gaze hardened and he opened his mouth but I fled. Back in my room I couldn't help but feel I'd lost something, maybe forever.

Zac found me in the kitchens. It was almost midnight; the night sky outside one of the steamy windows was peppered with stars. I was sitting at one of the benches, trying not to think about what I'd done.

"Ann?" he asked. I swivelled around immediately. "Yes?"

"I have a message for you."

I clambered off the bench and faced him. "From?"

"You know who. Don't mess around." He snapped at me. We were silent for a moment.

"What is it?" I began timidly.

"You need to trap some animals and bring them to him."

"Is that it?"

"Yes." There was another moment of tense silence.

But I couldn't stand it. "I'm sorry, Zac. I'm so sorry.
I know ..." but he cut through my babble.

"I don't want to hear it Ann. To be honest, I don't
care. I warned you, didn't I? I said that he'd try and
you promised you wouldn't ever work for him."
Every word stung with a painful truth.

"I know," I murmured, "but Bella." He spun around
wrathfully, "You can't even comprehend how many
people have died for that, to prevent what you've
given in to for the sake of your sister. His threats are
empty. You could have left this house if you really
were scared for her. You are scared for yourself.
You're a coward. A coward!"

"Do not blame me! You did exactly the same for
your family!" He froze, his face ridged with fury.

"They killed my family before that. They killed them
and they made me watch! I knew they would carry
out what they said they would do! I had seen proof.
He won't do that! He is not like them!"

Before he'd even finished spitting the last word at
me he'd disappeared, leaving me feeling hollow
and empty, all alone, in the middle of the echoing
kitchen.

§

The first animal I caught was a baby rabbit. I heard
it struggling in the trap before I saw it. The metal
jaws had fastened cruelly onto its back foot and it
was whimpering pitifully. I watched it for a moment,
twirling the sack in my hand. I wouldn't have taken
it had I not thought of Bella at that second. I took a
deep breath and mumbled, "It's only an animal, it's
only an animal." It didn't stop a huge lump rising
in my throat every time I felt it wriggle in the bag
on my back. Back in the house, I handed the sack
wordlessly to Charles. He lifted out the struggling

rabbit, holding it firmly by its ears. The rabbit uttered its terrified squeaks again. I felt a strange urge to knock it out of his hands and clenched my fists to conceal my feelings. He was examining the animal very carefully, and when he saw its crushed foot he lifted his eyebrows in surprise.

"Good trapping work," he commented. I looked at my hands. He put the rabbit back into the sack and laid it on the desk. I tried not to watch the sack twitching around on the desk, staring instead at a hole in the carpet. Charles reached across the table and picked up the key to the other door. Walking over to it, he unlocked and pushed it wide open.

"Bring the rabbit and come," he ordered and entered the room. Even though I never wanted to touch the sack again, I approached the table and picked it up gingerly.

"Hurry," came his impatient voice again. I followed him into the room. It was different since the last time I'd been there. The large wooden table had been pushed up against the far wall and barricaded in by three large chests positioned around it. The manacles hung from the wall, still shiny from Zach's cleaning. The small folding table stood in the centre of the room. Charles had his back to me, fiddling with something on the centre table. He looked up as I entered and held out his hand for the rabbit. I handed it over without complaint. On the table was the device he'd been perfecting a few days ago. Now a lighted candle stood in the candle holder, and the winch was in place. Charles laid the rabbit next to the device on the table and it quivered there, its foot still bent back horribly. He then moved the mirror over the top of the candle flame and a beam of dusty golden light suddenly lit the room. Charles paid me

no attention as he positioned the light just the way he
wanted it. Once he'd done that he seized the rabbit
and, before I could say or do anything, snapped its
neck with a sickening crack. If he heard my tiny
gasp he made no move. Instead he took the knife
and drew it across his middle finger, drawing blood.
I stood frozen as he let one drop fall onto the candle
flame; the light shining from the mirror darkened to
a deep scarlet. He ignored his still bleeding finger.
Taking hold of the mirror, he moved it so the light
bathed the dead rabbit's fur. It looked like the rabbit
was soaked in blood. I was clenching my fists so
hard that I felt my nails threaten to break the skin.
I watched as, right in front of me, the rabbit's foot
stopped bleeding. The bone clicked back into place
and the torn skin healed. And then it opened its
eyes; they flared red before subsiding into an ice
cold blue. They didn't look right, belong, in the face
of the rabbit with its soft brown face and twitching
whiskers. Charles watched warily as it lay there,
simply looking. Then something started seeping
from its fur, something that looked like smoke and
smelt like burning meat. Charles took out of his
pocket a locket, similar to the one Zac had given
me. He opened it cautiously and as if the smoke was
alive it responded, swaying grotesquely from the
rabbit into the locket. The rabbit's eyes flared red
again, its paws twitching as if longing to run away.
The locket closed and the rabbit flopped back down
onto the table, limp and dead again.

That was the first time. I told myself it would be the
last. But it wasn't. Of course it wasn't. I returned,
day after day, taking whatever animal I caught,
anything I caught. I didn't want to stay and watch

but I did; I hated myself for it. Soon, lines of lockets hung from the ceiling and my hands were ridged with cuts and scars. The first locket he'd given Zac was nowhere to be seen and I saw no trace of the cloth ropes either. Now I knew what was in there I knew the clothes I'd been tearing up must have belonged to her as well. He gave his blood the first time but in the end it was me. Always me. I said nothing anymore. Everything I did was wordless, only actions. I told myself that if I didn't speak, I could pretend it wasn't me. He gave me money too, more than I could have hoped for. And I took it; a small consolation, but consoling nevertheless. The only problem was, whenever I looked at it I saw the blood that had been spilt to get it, and I hated myself. If Bella noticed anything, she didn't say. If Lizzie noticed anything, she didn't seem to want to say. I smiled at them and turned up when I needed to in order to avoid questions but otherwise, I was alone. It was better that way. As long as Bella was hanging over my head, I didn't want her anywhere near him. And that meant I didn't want here anywhere near me. When I told Lizzie to look after her, I meant it. I no longer saw Zac. I'd heard he was working in the stables but could never pluck up the courage to go and see him. I couldn't bear his disgust on top of my own. He must hate me now. Everything he'd worked to stop, I was now assisting. The evil he'd fought so long I was now helping to breed and multiply. Sometimes I'd sit in the valley, hoping he'd turn up and, of course, he never did. The valley felt cold and empty now; everything seemed to have turned its back on me. I was helping to do things that should never be done, things that should have been left alone. Let the dead stay dead. But here they were alive again, and trapped for eternity in the gold lockets hanging in the hidden room. I think Lizzie still disapproved of my not going to church but she said nothing. How could I go to church, knowing what I was doing, day in, day out? How could I sit there, knowing I was committing a sin so willingly, with no thought for the consequences posed on my soul and pretend to pray? I would be a hypocrite to go. I would be a liar to go. I had lost so much self-respect anyway, anything I could claw a hold of, I held onto. Mrs Langley never even sent for me anymore. She sometimes gave me a pile of clothes, or something similar, to counter the suspicions of the others. I had friends now only for Bella, to keep the peace with Bella. There was no particular need for companionship.

The days flew past and the year passed too. We'd been here near on a year-and-a-half now. Spring and summer had passed in their turn. I wondered what I would have been doing if I hadn't come. There must have been other work somewhere. What about Bella? Would the two of us have been slaving in some field, growing fat and healthy on the produce of the land or would we be lying in some broken hovel, dead and cold and unknown? I often wondered. I knew I had changed when I saw my face in a bowl of water. I avoided looking at myself usually but accidentally caught a glimpse in the still water; I was immediately captivated by what I saw. My hair, which was straight anyway, hung lankly around my face and my eyes were huge black holes in my white face. When I tried smiling my mouth contorted into something between a grimace and a sneer. I was an ugly thing, with a wrinkled face and unsmiling mouth. My hair twisted into long rat-tails and felt coarse and broken. My beautiful hair was gone. Is that what people saw? I splashed my hands in the water so that I wouldn't have to look and turned away. But the memory of how I looked stayed printed in my mind. I couldn't get rid of it.

§

I knew what to do. Holding the knife firmly in one hand and clenching my teeth, I drew it carefully over my finger, refusing to gasp even when I felt the sting of pain. Charles watched with approval, and a hint of amusement.

"You've changed."

I inclined my head. "You make that sound like it's a good thing."

"Maybe it is," he returned. I had no answer for that. We had moved to the other room. A large fox hung in the manacles on the wall, its dead head lolling limply. I concentrated on dripping the blood onto the candle flame, watching it sizzle and the resultant deep scarlet of the light. Holding the mirror I shone the light onto the fox and stepped back, nursing my bleeding finger. Charles stood up from the chair he'd been lounging in and took my place behind the machine. I had come to hate that thing. The sheer wrongness of it shook me, the sheer power of it terrified me. Every dead animal that passed through its light awoke from the grip death held over it. Even death, the most powerful, the most certain thing we had, retreated before this thing, cowering and trembling. The fox twitched and started to fight the manacles. Charles watched, ready with the locket to capture the smoke that almost immediately started pouring from its rusty fur. As it emerged, it half formed the shape of a fox, snarling and snapping before surrendering to the pull of the locket. Charles left it on the table.

"May I go now?" He didn't answer; instead he moved the light so that it was facing the door. If anyone entered they would receive the full blast of it. It still burned a dark crimson. I looked at it with some trepidation and bemusement.

"You may in just a moment. First, I need to ask you something," and he returned to his chair.

"What?" He laughed. "You still hate me, don't you Ann?"

"How could I possibly not?"

He chuckled again and seemed to share a private joke with himself.

"Indeed, how could you not? But tell me, do you think this would work on humans?" Something hit me very hard in the stomach as I remembered Zac's sad story and his tribe. And then I remembered his sister.

"I asked you a question." I had lost my 'sirs' at the end of every line I said and, despite the fact he didn't seem to mind, he didn't waste a second making sure I knew who was in charge. As if I could ever forget.

"I don't know. Does this have something to do with the locket?"

"So you do know about it?"

I held my ground. "Yes."

"How much do you know about it?"

"Not a lot."

"I see. But the locket is not one of my great concerns at present. The question I asked is more pressing this time."

"I don't know."

"Are you sure the boy has not told you?"

"If he had told me, I would not tell you." For a moment, I wondered whether I had gone too far. But

Charles simply smiled again.

"I have a problem and was wondering if you could assist me." He was making fun of me. I knew it. After the dress came two other of his presents, two exquisite leather-bound books, each tied with a ribbon. Both had met their death in the fire before I had even opened them. The smell of burning paper had lingered in the room for days afterwards.

"What?"

"Would they need to be dead or alive?"

"You're the one with all the answers," I retorted, not caring what I sounded like. He raised his eyebrows. "Temper is never attractive, Ann." I glared at him. "And anyhow, I may be one with all the answers but this is one I don't know. Didn't the gypsy boy tell you anything?"

"If he had given me the answer, I wouldn't have told you anyway," I repeated through gritted teeth.

"Are you sure?"

"Yes."

Charles smiled a sinister smile. "I was afraid you would say that." Right at that moment, there was a faint tap on the door.

"Sir? Are you there?"

It was Bella's voice.

§

Before I could react, Charles pinned me up against him, clamping his hand so tightly over my mouth I struggled to breathe let alone shout. He dragged me out of view from the door and called out, "Yes? Come on in." I screamed futilely into his hand, thrashing in vain in his grip. I could only watch. And watch I did. The door opened slowly. I caught a fleeting glimpse of Bella standing there, arms full of clothing, before the light, the light that had not yet once failed, hit her bathing her in its glow. She froze. The clothes fell from her hands. I clawed at the hand smothering my mouth as I watched my beloved sister fall, as if through water, before hitting the ground. The crash sounded too loud and she lay too still, yet twitching slightly. She'd made no sound. Charles still wouldn't release me. All I could think of was that she was gone, that she was dead. I had killed her. I had killed Bella. He wouldn't let me go. Instead he dragged me across to the machine and blew out the candle. Finally, the light disappeared. I tore at his hand and at last he let me go. The scream that had been smothered escaped in all its shrill terror and anger.

"She's dead! You've killed her!" I screamed at him, running to her side.

"Bella! Bella! Please, wake up! Bella!"

Charles hadn't said a word. I shook Bella frantically but her head drooped onto her shoulder. She didn't respond.

"What have you done?" I shrieked. "What have you done?" Charles made a move towards her. I flung myself in front of her, shielding whatever was left of her from his murderous intention. He looked coolly down at me.

"Why are you blaming me? You wouldn't tell me what the gypsy boy said. You knew the answer. This is your fault." I couldn't help it. I burst into tears. Whether he spoke the complete truth or not, the stark logic in his words hurt.

"Bella?" I whispered through my tears. "Please wake up. Please."

I sat beside her on my bed, holding her cold hand in mine. I felt numb. Everything I'd done, everything

I hadn't, was because of this. The attic door opened and Lizzie came in. Her eyes fell on Bella and she let out a little cry.

"So, it's true? She's dead?"

"I don't know," I choked. "I don't know." And the tears came again. One look at my face and Lizzie was next to me. I hugged her as fiercely as she hugged me and cried into her shoulder.

"It's my fault," I sobbed. "It's all my fault."

"Why would it be your fault?"

But I couldn't tell her. Bella was still in danger. We couldn't go yet. And while she was here, she remained powerless in front of him. I was still powerless to protect her. I had to follow his rules. So I didn't answer. To my great relief, Lizzie didn't press me.

"She's not dead," I managed. "She's just ill. So ill." Lizzie moved around to the other side of the bed and took Bella's other hand, stroking it gently. I wiped the tears from my cheeks and a tear that had fallen onto her hand. 'Please wake up,' I begged her silently, willing her to open her eyes.

"What's the matter with her?" Lizzie solicited. I lifted my head and saw my feelings mirrored on her face: fear, grief and confusion. I shook my head hopelessly.

"Does Mrs Langley know?" she continued. I shook my head. Lizzie looked at me in amazement. "But she will help. She loves Bella. We should get help ..."

"No!" I shouted, surprising both of us. "They will not touch her."

"But they can help!" she implored.

"No!" I repeated stubbornly. "She will get better. They don't need to touch her." I wasn't about to let her become the new topic of gossip. I was going to guard her and protect her as I should have before. I refused to let him see I was so afraid for her; I wasn't going to sacrifice my pride. I'd keep this little bit. The three of us were silent. I found myself watching the rise and fall of Bella's chest, just to remind myself it had happened, to remind myself she wasn't dead. Her hair looked washed-out, her face had lost its rosiness. Her mouth was opened slightly and her feet twitched constantly under the blankets.

"You really love her, don't you?" I had been meaning to ask Lizzie this for some time. She started and looked up at me, then smiled rather sadly and nodded.

"Yes. I had a sister and brother once upon a time."

"Then where are they now?" I was shocked.

"I don't know," she admitted. "I was sent here when I was very young. They didn't want many extra hands and mouths to feed so I was the only one taken. Mother told me she'd send an address as to where they settled so I could go and see them, but I never got it. I received word that she'd died in a cart accident. I don't know what happened to the other two. Most likely dead." I digested this information in silence.

"I'm so sorry," I offered at last. She shrugged.

"Your sister and you reminded me of my sister, and of the life I could have had."

"You can still have that life," I returned. "You have Bella. She loves you very much, I can tell." Lizzie's beautiful blue eyes filled with tears.

"Not as much as she does you."

I lowered my head, embarrassed. "I don't know about that."

"It is," Lizzie promised me. "It is."

Lizzie went to church alone that week. Bella was still ill. For days she'd just laid there, her hair fanned out across the white pillows, her body still, so deathly still and pale. Whenever I slept I felt the chill radiating out of her, making me feel cold. I sat beside her long into the night, silently begging her to wake up. Lizzie told me repeatedly to tell Mrs Langley and ask for help, but I refused. No doctor with poking fingers and strange instruments and treatments would lay hands on her. If she was going to get better, she would. She wasn't ill. That much I knew. She'd been struck by something far deadlier than an illness. When Lizzie returned from church I was still sitting next to Bella, holding her hand.

"Ann, you should get out. You look dreadful."

"I'm not leaving her."

"I'll stay with her. Get some air. Go to your valley."

It was the first time I'd heard Lizzie say that. I looked at her open, worried face and nodded.

"Look after her." It wasn't a question. I didn't need an answer. I knew she would. I tied my hair up and left the room, clattering down the stairs. Lizzie was right. It was a beautiful day. It had rained the night before and now the earth smelt wet and fresh, birds sang joyfully and the wind blew merrily. As I passed Charles's window I kept my head bent, determined not to look, determined to drive him from my mind. Not even his money was worth the price I'd had to pay.

The valley was quiet. I took my usual spot among the grasses. Spring was returning. At that thought, a lump grew in my throat. I swallowed, shaking my head in annoyance. What was the matter with me? I hadn't cried a single tear for years and now they came nearly every day, unannounced and unwanted. So lost was I in thought I didn't notice the other person sitting some distance away, watching me. When I did notice, it was because it spoke.

"Hello. Ann?"

"Zac." He sat down beside me. We said nothing. I felt words would not break the awkwardness that hung between us.

"I heard about your sister," he offered.

"How?" I snapped. He merely looked at me, willing me to guess the answer. I looked away.

"I hate him."

"So do I," he agreed. "How is she? What happened?" I didn't answer.

"Ann?"

"It's all my fault," I managed, burying my head in my sleeve. I felt his hand on my arm.

"It's not. I'm sorry for what I said, Ann. I really am. I would have done the same thing."

"He tricked her. I couldn't warn her. He made me watch."

"He is a cruel man. That is what he does. That is what they all do." I lifted my face and looked at him. "How do you survive?"

Zac looked at me puzzled. "With what?"

"Your family. Knowing what they are, how they are yet you can do nothing. How do you survive?" His eyes twinkled with something I couldn't decipher.

"I believe," he replied simply. "I believe that tomorrow will be better, that tomorrow will bring answers that today couldn't find."

"But I can't find the answers. I can't work them out. And there are probably no answers for me anyway; there are no places I can go to find them."

"Wait," he offered. "They'll come to you instead."

"I can't. She's going to die Zac."

"We're all going to die, Ann."

"I don't want to do it anymore but Bella is too sick to leave. I'm trapped."

"You chose it, Ann," he reminded me gently.

"I don't want it now," I mourned. "I wish I'd never come here. I wish I was somewhere else, far away."

"So do I," he agreed. Again we sat in silence. Presently, I asked him nervously, "Do you hate me? For what I did?"

Zac gradually raised his head until his gaze was level with mine. "No Ann, I don't hate you. I hate what you're doing and hate that you gave in to him but no, I don't hate you."

"I'm sorry," I murmured, feeling even more wretched.

"Don't be sorry," he replied, burying his own face into his arm and adding, "there are things I wish I hadn't done too."

"That's different," I repudiated. "You had absolutely no choice. You did everything you could."

"Thank you, Ann." Neither of us spoke for a long while after that. We simply sat relishing the peacefulness in each other's company. Even the thought of Bella lying motionless couldn't drive away the happiness I felt at hearing that Zac didn't hate me, that I still had a true friend apart, from Lizzie, in this otherwise whirlwind of fear and cruelty.

"We should name this valley," Zac said decidedly. I sat up straighter, bemused.

"What do you mean?"

"Well, it doesn't actually belong to the house you know, and it doesn't belong to the forest. We should name it, mark it as our own because no one ever comes down here."

"Oh."

"Let's each mark out our name in the side of the valley, with the white stones in the river."

"I have a better idea," I rejoined. "Let's combine our names and make that instead. It belongs to both of us."

He grinned. "Race you to the water."

The water was icy cold. A strong current splashed around the black rocks poking out at intervals.

I gasped as I put my foot in and withdrew it immediately. Zac waded in almost to the middle and started gathering stones.

"I'll get them and you start making the letters," he suggested, picking up the smooth stones and collecting them in his shirt. I agreed, gratefully putting my shoes back on. Zac let the stones tumble onto the ground then went back for more. I filled my pockets and headed up the side of the valley a little. I started to lay out the letter Z. Zac trailed up again and again until there was a modest pile beside me, like a cairn on a mountain top. When he'd collected a fair few, he helped me lay out the A and the N. When we'd finished, he stepped back to admire it and nodded.

"It looks good." He smiled. I picked up one of the stones. It was oval and white and cold. The sun shone weakly but the river water still held the stones in its grip. As I held it, I thought of Bella. And as I thought of Bella, I realised I'd been away too long.

"I've got to go," I muttered apologetically. "I've got to be with my sister." His carefree face suddenly turned grave. "Ah, yes, of course. We'll both go back." From the top of the valley, I looked back.

The sun was starting to set but its golden light still shone over the stones; they glimmered faintly. While walking back I asked about the horse I'd seen him riding up the valley, the horse I now knew belonged to Sara.

"Nox? Yes, he's here. He stays in the stables mostly. They won't let me see him. They probably think I'm going to steal him again," he grumbled bitterly.

"Is that his name, Nox?"

"Yes. I named him that."

"It's a lovely name," I offered. He nodded in response. As we approached the house, I unconsciously looked up towards Charles' window. He followed my gaze.

"He's an evil man," he warned. We circled the wall to enter through the front gate.

"I know that now," I retorted, immediately regretting my harsh words. "I'm sorry. I don't mean to be like that."

"I'm just reminding you. Watch your sister and look after her. Goodbye, Ann."

"Goodbye, Zac."

§

I avoided the kitchen because of lots of noise and shouting coming from it. I wanted to see Bella. The feeling of lightness now in my heart didn't disappear, even as I climbed the stairs knowing what I'd see. I opened the door. Three pairs of eyes greeted me.

"Ann! Where have you been?" Mrs Langley's face was angrier than I'd ever seen it. Bella still lay motionless on the bed but Lizzie had moved away from her and was folding clothes on her bed. Even from the doorway I could see the deep red blush spreading up Lizzie's pale neck and cheeks.

The realisation of what had happened hit me like a hammer. Mrs Langley was still glowering at me. "Where have you been?" she repeated. I ignored her. Feelings of rage were curdling in my stomach. I had trusted her. I had trusted Lizzie to look after Bella. How could I have been so stupid? I never should have left her. Brushing past Mrs Langley, I rushed to Bella. There was a clean white bandage on her arm and a bottle of some sort of cordial on the floor beside her.

"Elizabeth here told me this girl was very sick and we sent immediately for the doctor." I said nothing. I could not trust myself to speak. Mrs Langley continued, "We will have to move her downstairs."

"No!" I shouted. The thought of Bella lying still and cold in some fancy bedroom downstairs, far away from me, was more than I could bear.

"Ann, you have no choice in this matter!" barked Mrs Langley. "You have already shown you do not care for her, enough to leave your friend to look after her while you go gallivanting off somewhere." Lizzie had the good sense to stay quiet.

"She does not need a doctor's help," I spat out through gritted teeth. "She does not need anyone to help her. She needs to stay here with me."

"This decision is final," snapped Mrs Langley. "Your lack of care is atrocious. She could have died. The doctor said she was in a critical condition anyway, and this attic will not help her get any better."

"Then I am coming too," I answered obstinately. "She's my sister and you cannot, and will not, take her away from me." Mrs Langley looked like she was going to argue but then, taking another look at my blazing eyes and my hand gripping Bella, nodded grudgingly.

"You may come. But she must go." I knew another
decision would not be reached. After that, things
moved very quickly. Mrs Langley had summoned
one of the kitchen staff to help us move everything
downstairs. There wasn't a lot. He took the chest
and so I moved to pick up Bella. I wouldn't let
anyone else hold her. She weighed next to nothing.
Lizzie was to stay behind. Before leaving I shot
her a look of disgust. She stood in the middle of
the room, looking lost and imploring. I didn't care.
Without her, none of this would have happened.
She didn't care about me. She thought she knew the
best for Bella and had gone behind my back to trick
me. Medicine wouldn't cure her, I knew, because
she wasn't sick. She had something far worse than
a disease. And I couldn't tell. We stopped at one
of the rooms on the third floor. As we strode the
corridor that led to Charles's study I couldn't help
but look along it. The door was shut. I hurried past.
Bella's head rested against my shoulder, her hands
lying on her stomach. She was still dressed in the
long grey dress she'd been wearing when hit by the
light. I tried not to think about it. It hurt too much.
The room we were allocated was much larger than
the attic and much grander. But there was so much
colour it hurt my eyes; so much red; a red carpet
on the floor and huge bunches of roses on the
windowsill and on top of the hope chest. Their scent
was strong and cloying. The bed was vast and hung
with scarlet drapes and covered with a heavy ruby
duvet. All the wood in the room was polished to
perfection and had a red tint. The sky outside was a
dull black. I couldn't see the stars.
"You will stay here," Mrs Langley ordered. "You
will not move from this room and you will not take

her anywhere, do you understand?" I nodded, still holding tightly onto Bella. No one was going to take her away from me, not Mrs Langley, not Lizzie, not anyone. Mrs Langley gave me another piercing, disapproving look.

"I am very disappointed in you." She swept out of the room. I walked across the carpet, disliking its soft, spongy feel. I put Bella on the bed. She looked lost in all its fine draperies. The poles supporting the canopy were thick and gnarled, like great tree trunks. The feet of the bed ended in curved claws. On the wall hung a picture of a battle. Horses bared their teeth and reared, their heads crowned with large, barbed-like plumes. Men bellowed from atop them or writhed on the blood-soaked ground. The sky was full of crows that cawed, and even in the dim light their swords and bayonets glinted. I returned to the bed and picked up Bella's hand.

"I'm sorry Bella. I really am. I don't know why I brought you here away from the safety of home. This is not a good place to be in and the minute you get better, we're leaving. We're going far away and never coming back. Maybe we'll go to the town. Would you like it there? We'll go together. Please, Bella, open your eyes." I brushed a strand of hair from her face and rubbed her cold hand with mine, trying to generate some warmth.

"Do you remember our parents? How they worked so hard to make things happy? Do you remember the toys they made for you there? Do you remember the dolls? It was a good life Bella. I promise you, we'll have that life again, that it will be ours. When you get better."

The duvet crushed us under its weight. I lay in the

dark listening to Bella's faint breathing beside me. Had it not been for that I'd have thought she was dead. She looked dead. She felt dead. But she was alive. I held her hand under the blanket despite its coldness, its death-like feel. I was used to death now. Just not in my sister. I dreamt that night. I dreamt I'd floated out of my body and was looking down at myself from the ceiling, down on my frowning face and Bella's peaceful one. I was watching us when the door opened; someone concealed beneath a long black cape crept inside. I watched anxiously as the person peered at the sleeping me, then moved around to the other side of the bed and stood next to Bella. My heart beat faster as the person began searching in the long cape for something, eventually bringing out a tiny glass vial. I couldn't see what was in it; it was too dark. The person unstopped it and trickled its contents over Bella's mouth. A fine dust-like substance floated dreamily out and across her half-opened lips. She immediately began to cough and move. A glowing colour returned to her cheeks and her eyes flew open. I let out a silent cry when I saw them blaze red. The stooped, cloaked figure rustled out of the room. Bella was still coughing in bed. My sleeping figure wouldn't move. Abruptly, I felt a tugging sensation along my spine and I sped towards my sleeping body. The two halves of me fused and I sat up, very much awake. The coughing continued.

"Ann?" I heard a wispy voice beside me. I spun round.
"Bella? Oh Bella! You're awake!" She was lying there, eyes half open and she had a hacking cough. Pushing the dream to the back of my mind, I fetched some water from the enamel wash basin and sat

beside her, holding her head to help her drink.

"Ann, I had a horrible dream," she whimpered, after she'd finished drinking and the coughing had subsided.

"I know," I soothed. "But you're awake now, and that's what matters." She struggled to sit up so I propped another cushion under her head.

"Where are we?"

"We're in another bedroom on the third floor. You've been asleep for so long and we were all very worried about you. What can you remember?" Her gaze clouded with confusion.

"I don't know," and her voice still weak and croaky. "I remember carrying clothes somewhere and opening a door and lots of light and it hurt. It hurt so much, Ann." She began crying again. I picked her up in my arms and hugged her.

"I know. But we're going away, far away from this place, do you understand? We're going to leave. Nothing will ever hurt you again." She carried on crying on my shoulder. "Try and sleep now," I encouraged, putting her back gently onto the covers. I covered her with the blanket and took her hand. The beautiful colour was returning to her cheeks. But then, just as she was being dragged under she murmured sleepily, "And there was a man, a very rich man."

I froze. "What man?"

"I don't know. He said he would give me many pretty things if I helped him. He showed me some of them."

I took her by the shoulders. "Listen to me, Bella. Listen! He is a very dangerous person. If you ever see him again, don't speak to him and don't listen to him, do you understand?" I tightened my grip on her shoulders. I was so scared. How long had he known her? How long had she spoken to him? Had she been helping him as well? The answers were too frightful to think about. Bella's blue eyes widened slightly as she looked up at me.

"Promise me Bella! Promise me you'll do as I say!"

"I promise Ann." And then she was asleep again.

§

She was not out of danger; that much I knew for certain. I was not naïve enough anymore to think that she was safe but still I couldn't drive my dream out of my head. Had that really happened? Or had it been a dream? I couldn't tell the gender of the figure, the height, the shape. Everything was concealed. And I knew now that ignorance, in this house, was not bliss. Bella was instructed to remain in the room we'd been give and I, of course, refused to leave her. I also refused to help him. Every morning after that, I would return to the kitchen, as before, to be assigned my list of chores. Mrs Langley treated me with permanent disdain. Her harsh nature hardened even more and became an open face of disgust. She would constantly criticize and overlook my work, making fun of me and blaming me for everything. I understood her a little though. She couldn't comprehend why on earth I hadn't told her when Bella had first become sick. If I were truly honest with myself, I didn't understand either; I just knew I hadn't wanted to. She was mine. On the other hand, Lizzie was in a constant state of submission and guilt whenever she saw me in the corridor or elsewhere. Perhaps she really did feel concerned for Bella's welfare but I couldn't forgive her. The small grain of trust I'd handed her she'd tossed away; I wasn't stupid enough to give her another. She wasn't resentful of my blanking; instead it seemed to make her even more apologetic. She knew she'd done wrong and I, in my state of worry and anger, let her linger in her pit of shame. I was serious about leaving but couldn't bring myself to give notice until Bella was completely better. What I couldn't stop were the frequent visits of the doctor, coming with his strange medicines and instruments, armed to the teeth with knives and saws. Whenever he came I adamantly stayed in the room with Bella. Lizzie hadn't been able to stop him but I was more than capable. He could look at her but could not touch. I wished I'd that much power over everyone in the house.

As I'd returned to normal duties, I came back at around midnight, occasionally later. Mrs Langley seemed to grab every opportunity to make my life harder and harder, working me from dawn to dusk, maybe as punishment, maybe as jealousy. Today I'd been in the gardens and the wash house, as far away from the house as I could get. I knew she wanted to make sure I knew my place; I was merely a servant here and I did know it. Bella had stayed up, waiting for me. I didn't know if Lizzie had come to visit her, I didn't know if Lizzie even knew where we were. Sometimes I thought of her, sleeping alone upstairs by herself, but I only had to remind myself of what she'd done and I could quench any wavering flames of sympathy.

"Do you feel any better?" Bella nodded but averted her gaze. I felt a quick stab of suspicion.

"Bella? What is it?"

"Nothing." She smiled, but it was a pained smile. I scrutinized her carefully and noticed she was holding her side rather tightly. I felt a flicker of fear.

"What happened, Bella? What did you do?"

"Nothing," she repeated, biting her lip, a sure sign she was lying.

"Bella, show me!" She was still obedient, even to me, and took her hand away little by little. There was a fresh bandage wrapped around her middle.

"Who did that to you?" I jumped onto the bed for a closer look. She bit her lip again.

"Tell me, Bella. I won't let anyone know you told."

"He did," she whispered. I didn't need to know anymore.

"When?"

"Today, maybe an hour ago. He gave me this," and she reached under her pillow and brought out a little ribbon, the span of my thumb, just long enough to tie a bow. It was bright yellow and fringed with red. I could easily see why Bella wanted it. She loved ribbons.

"Just that?" She nodded nervously. I started for the door then stopped. I was torn. I didn't want to leave Bella but I wanted revenge. Bella watched me apprehensively from the bed.

"What are you going to do?" I started again for the door handle.

"Leave me alone Bella!" I growled furiously. Something in my chest roared for revenge. She recoiled from the look on my face. The ribbon hung limply from her hand, feigning innocence. With a barely contained snarl, I snatched it from her.

"What did he say?" I demanded. "What did he say to you?" Bella was visibly shaking but I was past caring. Was he going to take everything from me? Even though he'd promised?

"He said he'd give me a present," she stammered, "If

I gave him something back."

"And then?"

"I don't remember," she stammered, hanging her head. "I think I went to sleep. When I woke up, the bandage was there and so was the ribbon." She lifted her head to look at it, then looked at me. Her lip trembled at the barely-concealed derision on my face.

"It was so pretty." I stamped my foot.

"He's dangerous! I told you! You promised me you'd leave him alone!"

Her face crumpled. "I'm sorry Ann." At the sight of her tears my anger vanished. It wasn't her fault. Hadn't I also fallen for his clever words and plentiful gifts? The large gold coins in my chest were proof of that.

"Bella, I don't mean to get angry. I'm scared for you, that's all. You don't need this ribbon. You'll find another one somewhere. Ask Mrs Langley the next time you see her. Just leave him alone. He is dangerous. You must leave him alone! Sleep now, alright? We'll sort this out in the morning."

Bella sniffled and buried her head into my shoulder. "Do you forgive me, Ann?"

"Of course," and I kissed the top of her head goodnight. She fell asleep soon after. I stayed awake, thinking and plotting.

§

I didn't bother to knock. I knew he was there. As I barged in, he looked up, quietly assessing me with cool eyes. The machine was nowhere to be seen. It must be in the other room.

"What did you do to my sister?" He sat back in his chair.

"I simply did what she let me do," he replied. "I

wouldn't have done anything if she hadn't let me."

"She's a child!"

"She's old enough to know what she wants."

"Just because she wants it doesn't mean she should get it."

"Ah, is that your policy? If she wants food, she should necessarily have it? If she wants a family, she shouldn't necessarily have it?" I struggled for something to say. "You know that's not what we're talking about."

"Isn't it?" He stood up and looked me over. "I don't think you have any power over her body and blood. What I took was hers to give away or keep. She is not your slave."

"She is my sister!"

"Exactly. How much time have you spent with her recently? Does it take a near-death experience for you to notice that?"

"I knew it," I denied. I told myself he was twisting my words but, on the other hand, I could see the sense in what he was saying, the truth in his words. How much time had I really spent with Bella? Not a lot. I'd guarded her against people that could help her. I'd kept her away from people who could have helped her. I'd dragged her all over the countryside with me on mad chases that may have or may not have worked. She'd said nothing so I'd assumed she was alright. The minute I thought all of this, I shook my head. He'd put it in there, like he'd done with Bella. I clenched my fists.

"Get out of my head," I hissed at him. He laughed. "I wish I was in your head. It would be very interesting, I think."

"Leave me alone."

"I haven't done anything. If you'd really hated

everything you did, you wouldn't have come back. You'd have left. You and I are not that different, you know. We're both fascinated by the things that lie just outside our reach."

"We are not alike," I hissed. "There is nothing similar about us. I did what I did because I was protecting my sister."

"But you kept her in the house when you could have left."

"And gone where?" I insisted. "I wouldn't have taken her out, back to the starvation we'd left." He didn't reply. Instead, he walked towards the other door.

"Come here."

"No." I took a step back. "I'm not helping you do anything anymore. You broke your promise."

He chuckled. "As you wish. I would come though, if I were you."

"But you are not," I pointed out. He inclined his head.

"That is true." And he entered the other room. Pride fought curiosity. In the end I moved reluctantly towards the door. Reaching out a hand I pushed it open. And stopped. Lying on the floor, unconscious, was a young boy, maybe my age or a bit younger. My eyes travelled to the table. There stood the machine, lit and ready. Charles stood behind it, his face indifferent and resolved. A locket hung from his hand, swinging gently. He was going to try again.

"No," I said faintly. He didn't move.

"Yes, I thought you might find this interesting."

"What have you done?"

"He will wake up. In time."

"You're a cruel man." I was biting the inside of my lip so hard I felt the skin split. The coppery taste of blood filled my mouth.

"That's your opinion. But enough talk. Think of your sister and do what you have to do." I shook my head. "I won't help you. I won't kill him. I'm not a murderer. I'm not like you. And you won't hurt my sister again."

"Won't I?" I shook my head dumbly. I had no idea where I was going with this. "How do you know?" he smiled, his little sinister smile, the smile snakes smile.

"You need her," I replied boldly. "She was one of your experiments, wasn't she?"

"Ah yes, I haven't shown you my latest discovery, have I?" Feeling around in his pocket he brought out a little coloured bottle. "I have everything I need." He shook the bottle gently. I heard liquid slosh and swallowed down bile as I realised what was in it.

"Therefore you won't hurt her anymore if you have everything you need." I was clutching at straws. That was what I'd turned into, someone clutching at straws. His eyes glinted mockingly.

"Are you asking me or telling me?" he taunted. I didn't have an answer. He pressed on.

"And anyway, is she the only person you care about in this house? What about this?" He turned and opened a large cupboard. He held Zac by the scruff of his neck. Reaching for the table, he picked up the knife lying there.

"So, what now, Ann?" Zac's eyes bore into mine. They were full of fear. I couldn't bear that look. But I couldn't kill that boy. And I couldn't let Charles do it either.

"Zac," I breathed. He struggled in Charles' grip.

"You won't do anything," I burst out recklessly.

A low sound of amusement sounded in the back

of Charles' throat. "Won't I?" Yanking Zac's hair to one side, he placed the blade almost casually there. It was so sharp a small cut appeared when he shifted it slightly. Zac gave me another look, pleading with me in a way he'd never done before.

"Ann, please." I jumped at the sound of his voice. It was not fearful. It was just resigned. Charles spoke again. "You need to make a choice. One will die. You decide which."

Zac shouted out suddenly. "He's lying! He's going to kill us all anyway. Get out! Leave!" His words ended in a gasp as Charles moved the knife again, and blood trickled down his neck.

"Please," I begged. "Please let them go. They haven't done anything wrong." He looked at me impassively. Zac, regardless, it seemed, of the knife pressing into his neck, continued struggling. The more he moved, the more the knife tugged and scratched at his skin.

"Zac, what do I do?"

"What's the matter?" Charles jeered. "Can't even make your own decision?"

"Let them go!" I implored. "Please let them go! I'll do anything. Just please leave them alone."

"Ann, no! Get out of here! Leave and take your sister with you! He will not keep his word!" Charles ignored him, fixing his eyes on me.

"Anything?"

"Anything," I agreed fervently.

"Ann, no!" Zac continued to shout and struggle.

"Stop it! Don't do that to yourself!" I hardened my resolve. "If you let them go, I will do anything. If you make a promise to leave Bella alone as well, I will do anything."

"You have my word." And he threw Zac to the floor.

"Leave him," he commanded. I'd instinctively started towards him and I forced myself to stop. Zac lay, panting slightly on the ground, looking up at me. He addressed me as if no one else was in the room. "What have you done, Ann? What have you done?"

On returning to my room several hours later I found Lizzie and Bella talking happily together.

"What is she doing here?" I demanded. Lizzie jumped and scrambled off the bed, wringing her hands. I strode into the room.

"Where have you been?" Bella asked.

"Outside. I went to the valley," I shot back. "What is she doing here?"

"I came to see Bella," explained Lizzie, carefully looking anywhere but at me.

"I don't want you here," and I took a purposeful step forward. "You don't belong here."

"Ann, what's wrong?" asked Bella from the bed. "What's the matter with you?"

"It's her!" I shouted. "It's all her!"

Lizzie cowered beneath my glare but said nothing.

"She's the reason we're stuck here, waiting for you to get better." I was speaking lies. They were all monstrous lies but I wanted to blame someone, I wanted to blame someone I could hurt.

"Ann, stop it!" cried Bella, horrified. I ignored her.

"You tricked me!" I accused. "I trusted you! I trusted you with the most precious thing I have and you tricked me!"

Lizzie still said nothing. This filled me with even more rage. Her face was terrified and ugly with shame. Furiously, I stalked towards her.

"Ann stop!" screeched Bella from the bed, struggling out from under the covers.

"Stop! What are you doing?"

She leapt in front of Lizzie. As her feet hit the ground her knees buckled from disuse and she could barely stand. Even this did not bring me to my senses.

"What's wrong, Ann? What's wrong?"

"Get her out of here!" Bella grabbed my arm but I threw her to the floor. Anger pulsed through my veins. I hated everything. I hated him, for all his twisted wishes and words. I hated Lizzie, for standing there so humbly and resignedly. I hated Zac for being so right. I even hated Bella for standing in the way, stopping my rage from exploding. But most of all, I hated myself. For everything I had tied myself to, for everything I had to do now, for everything I'd done.

"Get out!"

Lizzie fled. I ignored Bella, lying on the floor, and clambered instead into the bed myself, hiding my head in the pillow. Moments later I felt the mattress sink beneath another weight and a little hand started stroking my hair. I twisted away but the hand came right back, smooth, soothing strokes that calmed down even my anger.

"What happened?" she asked, rubbing my back. "Where did you go?"

"I went to the valley," I replied, still burying my face into the comforting warmth of the pillow.

"Before that, what happened?"

"He's a monster, Bella. He wanted me to kill someone. He had Zac. And I promised to do anything he told me if he let them go." I felt the hand still for a minute but then carry on as before.

"But why Ann? Why? Why were you so horrible to Lizzie? I thought you were friends."

"When you were ill, she told me she'd look after you; instead, she summoned Mrs Langley. She knew I didn't want anyone to see you. I didn't want the doctor to see you." The hand moved away.

"Didn't you want me better?"

"No Bella. That wasn't it. I wanted you better more than anything. But you were not ill. He had done something to you and I knew medicine wouldn't make you better. Medicine would do nothing to help you."

"I see," she murmured, resuming the stroking of my hair.

"Do you?" I asked. Her face was shaded with shadow. She looked so much older than nine. She nodded slowly.

"I'm scared Ann," she said finally, nuzzling down next to me. "What does he want to do?"

"He wants to try what he is doing on humans," I said. Whenever I thought it, fear clenched my stomach and bile rose in my throat. I had hopefully secured Bella's safety but my self-preservation instinct had disappeared.

"What will you have to do?"

"Help him in any way he wants me to," I supplied listlessly.

"But you won't have to kill someone, will you?"

For some time I didn't answer, thinking things over in my head. I didn't know where that boy had come from and I didn't know who he was. But I couldn't and wouldn't kill him. Charles had said I was like him but I refused to believe it. Everything he did was purely for his own aim. I had different hopes and wishes. My mouth automatically formed the word 'no' but then I remembered Charles' words and instead whispered to the dark of the room, "I don't know. I just don't know."

§

I closed my eyes, locked away my conscience, and did as he said. The light was a darker colour, more of a purple now, and its deadly speed and strength dispatched anyone or anything that crossed its path. I avoided looking into their eyes. If I didn't look in their eyes I might be able to convince myself they were animals, like before. Chained in the manacles they looked like animals. And we treated them like animals. Many a person would go missing in the village through my hands. I didn't know where they came from but knew where they ended up. He made me do things more for his own entertainment than anything else and would say smugly at the end, when another locket had been filled and another body destroyed, "You see? We're not so different after all."

"We are. You had a choice and I didn't." To which he would reply with a laugh, "Indeed."

He had the locket out again. It was appearing more and more recently. Sitting behind his desk he examined it very carefully, brushing off any dust he spotted. When I opened the door, he looked up. Sometimes he'd just let me get on with it so I started to walk towards the door. But he called me back.

"Not today, Ann. This is more important."

I stopped by the door. Standing up, he picked something up off the ground at his feet and lifted it slowly, holding it carefully, as if it was dangerous. It was a chest. Much smaller than the chest I had in my room but quite a bit taller. From the side I could see numerous deep carvings in the wood.

"What is that?"

He looked up at me. "Nothing, yet. We are going to

make it into something." He fetched the machine from the other room and cleared a space for it on his desk. I backed toward the other wall, out of its way.

"Scared, Ann?"

"I have a right to be. That thing should be destroyed." He grinned. "If that is your opinion, well, that is a pity. But I am not going to destroy it and you don't know how." Silence was my greatest weapon. I used it often to defend myself. Charles pointed to the corner behind the machine and I scurried there. He lit the candle and positioned the mirror over the top of the flame. He gestured to the light.

"We're going to try and capture this in the chest. The light will not be able to get out of there. I have made sure of that."

"Why?" I asked before I could stop myself. The last thing I wanted to do was to show interest in his little experiment but this had sparked my curiosity. Duly, I waited for some sort of mockery but it never came. He was staring at the light, turning his hand in its golden glow.

"With this light we see now, I cannot yet save my sister." It was weird hearing him talk about his sister. It showed another side of him, one I'd never seen before. When he spoke about his sister I was reminded just how young he was. He wasn't that much older than me. When I caught myself thinking like that, I shook my head. He didn't deserve thoughts like that.

"Why don't you just open it?" I asked, without really thinking. He flashed me a look, straightened, picked up the locket from his desk and held it out to me.

"Try to open it then." I took it gingerly. It was a long time since I'd held it in my hands.

"It's warmer," I muttered. The metal was now almost burning my skin. Charles nodded.

"I've been holding it in the light often. I thought perhaps that would help it open but it did nothing but warm up the metal. Try and open it." I pushed the clasps off the metal and tugged at the two halves. It was stuck.

"I can't," and I handed it back.

"I thought not. The light needed to open this needs to have been contained for some time. The light needed to open it needs to be trapped, and then we may release it. Hopefully, the force of that will open the locket."

"That's ridiculous. You can't trap light."

"But this light," he said, "this light is not like other types of light, is it? This light is different." He picked up the chest and handed it to me. There was not one smooth section on it. Its entire surface was covered in scratches and carved lines. On one side was the word Alpha and on the other, Omega. Above them were their symbols, whittled deep into the sides.

"And this will trap it?" I asked cautiously.

"Yes. With the right measures." He took out of his pocket the little bottle of blood he'd shown me before ... Bella's. I turned my eyes away as he opened it and carefully dropped three drops of the crimson liquid onto the candle flame. The light flashed a brilliant white and then dimmed into black. Black light. To raise the dead. This light made no shadow, seeming almost solid. I couldn't see the other wall through it. Charles' face lit up and his eyes widened. "Open the chest Ann," and I did. The light flashed on and off, with such brightness and intensity that I turned my head away and held the chest out.

"No, look! Look!" Charles ordered, his own eyes fixed on the scene in front of him. The light was writhing like a pit of snakes, coiling and uncoiling. As I watched the side appeared to shatter, pieces flew off the edge and embedded themselves into the side of the chest. From there they were sucked into the chest. The speed and size of the pieces grew and grew but all found their way into the chest. It grew heavier and heavier in my arms and when Charles at last said I could close it I staggered slightly before slamming the lid shut. The minute I had it closed he came up behind me and took it off me. Setting it on the table he picked up the knife and placed his hand out over the box. I realised what he was going to do a fraction of second before he actually did it. The knife sliced open his palm; his face expressionless as blood poured from his palm onto the carved roof of the chest. Before the blood could spill over its edge the wood greedily absorbed it. His face lit up. Ignoring the cut on his hand he picked up the chest, kicked open the other door and walked inside. I left an hour later, while there was still no answer from the other room.

§

Sunday again. The weeks passed too slowly. The days passed too slowly. Every hour dragged out with some new horror, something new to hate. We weren't allowed to return to our attic room, for which I was glad. I didn't want to see Lizzie. The tension between us had reached an agonizing peak. Bella may have felt more sympathy towards me because I was her sister, and we'd been through too much to abandon each other but Lizzie was her friend and she refused to speak of her with contempt as I did. I was disgusting in my sins. My shoulders hunched under the burden of the lives I carried and lines were etched into my face. While Bella flowered, I withered. But, again, if anyone noticed they said nothing. There was nothing to be said, nothing to be done. And Sunday had come again. Bella went to church. She wasn't obliged to work yet but she did want to go to church. With Lizzie. I headed for the valley as usual. Once there I could pick up the stones, look at the woods and imagine a life that could have been mine if it weren't for all my mistakes. Once outside I started running, gathering up my skirt so I could run faster. Run away, I told myself. Run away from him. From his dark eyes and mocking smile. From the room full of blood. From the room full of nightmares. The grounds were deserted. The fields were deserted. But when I got to the valley, I no longer felt safe. The letters Z-A-N stood out among the green grass and at the sight of them I felt tears welling up inside me. Zac. Bella. How many more people would I have to sacrifice everything for? How many more people would he destroy before he had what he wanted? I buried my head on my knees, gasping and soaking my dress with tears. I heard a crackling sound but didn't look up, still too wrapped up in my own misery. It wasn't until I felt someone sit down beside me that I looked up and screamed. A woman sat beside me ... but she was transparent. I could see the grass and the trees and the river. But I could see her pale waxen skin and big blue eyes. She wore a long green dress with a faint pink stain on the bodice; I stared at it, horrified. I swallowed rapidly as she smiled and reached out to touch my arm. Clapping my hand over my mouth I scrambled backwards, choking on fear.

"Hello, Ann," she said, in a whispery voice.

"Who are you? What do you want?"

"I'm Tess," she said, still smiling, "and I'm here to warn you."

"Of what? What are you? You're dead, aren't you?" I knew I was babbling but I couldn't think straight. Tess continued smiling, a smile with real warmth but looking creepy on the face of a dead thing.

"Yes, I am dead. I am Zac's mother. It's time to warn your Master."

"He's not my Master," I snapped vehemently. "He's a monster."

"Whether that is the case or not, he is still your Master," she continued smoothly. "You must warn him. The souls in the woods have become good. You must tell him this." She said that like it was a bad thing.

"I'm sorry but I have to go. I won't sit here and talk to a ghost." I pushed myself to my feet and started walking towards the house again. Tess re-appeared in front of me. I gave a muffled shriek.

"Why are you scared, Ann? You're living in a house with the dead. You're making and helping to make others dead like me. Why are you scared of me? Now listen. The spirits were bad, they are meant to be bad but now they are good. That means someone has summoned a lot of bad from everywhere around. We know it is him. You must tell him to get rid of it." The image of the chest rose in my mind but I rejected it.

"I don't know what you're talking about."

"If he releases that evil, everyone in your house becomes like me, guilty and innocent, man and woman, servant and Master. Everyone. Do you understand? You must tell him. Tell him to get rid of it. Tell him to destroy it."

"He doesn't listen to me. It's no good," I shouted. "I'm his slave, his pet, one of his experiments."

"You have more power than you know," she contradicted.

"You're dead," I fumed. "You wouldn't know."

"I have a son," she returned. "A son who is very close to you. I know the power you have. It is more than you realise. More than you want. The choice isn't yours to make. You must tell him."

"I will try," I grumbled.

"But he may not listen. I would try myself if I knew what it was but I cannot help you. He shares nothing with me. You must try. Otherwise everyone in that house is doomed." She disappeared.

That night I lay in the dark of the room, staring up at the canopy above me. Bella wasn't asleep but she left me alone as I turned over in my mind everything Tess had said. What would Zac say? What would Zac do? The spirits had turned good, she'd said. Did that mean his family was free at last? Would he return to them and leave me here?

"I wish," I started and then stopped, afraid to voice it. Bella turned to me in the dark.

"What do you wish?" It came out in a sudden rush. "I wish there was someone out there to take everything away from me. I wish someone would come along and save me. I wish he would pick on someone else for a change. Someone different. Someone who is not me."

"How do you know that won't happen?" came the quiet reply. "I don't. That's why I wish it."

While Bella slept quietly next to me I stayed awake, staring at the door without really seeing it. That chest held pure evil. Evil greater than I think even I could possibly imagine. And yet, he was doing it for his sister. To help her, get her out of that locket. Before Bella had fallen ill I'd have said it was impossible, that he should have just thrown it away but now, now I thought differently. As I lay there I thought about Zac and the first time I'd seen him all those months ago. He knew things that, back then, I wouldn't have ever dreamed of. If I'd been given a choice, back then, to learn the things I now knew, would I have taken it? Would I have seized the chance to raise from the dead anyone I wanted, would I have taken the chance to make anyone I wanted immortal? My thoughts immediately drifted to my family and then Bella. If I hadn't known the consequences, would I have tried to make her immortal? So that she'd never get ill, never feel pain, never die? Probably. Did that make me any different? I tossed and turned, trying to rid my head of these troublesome thoughts. You haven't killed anyone, I told myself firmly. You've been doing what you've been told. To protect the people you love. To protect Bella. I twisted around to look at her, to remind myself of the reason. But still, I did want someone else to come, to be what I was to him, to be his toy, the thing he could order around at will. I didn't want it to be me anymore.

§

The next week I was sent to the village. Apart from a large church, it was a poor and lowly place. The rich people lived in manor houses, like Fitz Hall, whereas the poor stayed in the village. Everyone knew each other, therefore unsurprisingly, strangers were treated with not a little suspicion. I hadn't been to church and hadn't often been sent here. I wasn't known, unlike Lizzie and Bella. The cart that carried me there was returning at midday, and I finished all my chores with one whole hour to spare. I went to the church graveyard and walked up and down the small allotments, reading the names on the worn wooden crosses and elaborate headstones. I stopped when I recognized a name … Sara; Sara Fitz, Charles' sister. An angel leant up against the tall curved cross, weeping tears onto its polished surface. Another angel knelt in front of the cross, also crying. I examined it from several angles. In its own macabre way it was beautiful. Looking down at the ground in front of the headstone, I wondered whether Sara Fitz did lie beneath that earth or was her corpse still in the forest in the valley with Zac's tribe. Did she know what was happening? Did her soulless body want a resurrection, want to revive? None of this would have happened without her. But I couldn't hate the dead body under my feet. She was trapped, just like me. We were the same.

The cart journey back was uneventful. Arriving at the house, the first thing I noticed was, all the curtains had been drawn and the shutters closed. No one in sight, not even a gardener. A sense of foreboding tickled my sixth sense. I entered through the servant's door, puzzled by something I couldn't quite put my finger on. Once inside the deserted kitchen, I became conscious of what it was; the place was empty. But it was mid afternoon and middle of the week, someone should have been there.

"Hello?" I called, hearing my lone voice echo. Hearing the servant's door open and close I backed up against the counter and picked up a carving knife behind me. After a few moments, Tess came in. She looked at the knife, amused.

"What use is that against a ghost?" she pointed out.

I ignored the joke. "Where is everyone?"

The teasing smile left her face. "Did you warn him?"

"I warned him but he didn't listen. I knew he wouldn't listen."

Tess stared at me for a moment then fired out, "Where is his study? Where does he do all his experiments?"

"This way," I nodded to the stairs and took them myself two at a time. The serious look on her face scared me like nothing else could. Before reaching the study, I crashed into our room. Bella was nowhere to be seen.

"Bella! Where is she? What has he done?" The blankets were crumpled, her sewing lay abandoned on the floor. Tess stood in the doorway.

"It's as if she was called," she whispered ominously. My head snapped around.

"Where's the study, Ann?"

"Where's my sister?"

"We must go to the study. We must stop him."

"Where is everyone?" She simply looked at me.

"We must go to the study, Ann." I dashed out the room and down the corridor, crashing through the halls and doorways as if they weren't there, trying to get to Bella before anything happened. At the study door, I stopped and seized the handle. I couldn't open it.

"Charles? Hello?" I called through the door. I put my ear to the wood. Except for a small clicking sound there was silence within. Click. Click. Click. Like a clock. Quietly. Preciously. Click. Click. Click. Then silence. Suddenly I was blown backwards into the wall, cracking my head against the wood. I heard Tess cry out then blackness embraced me. When I opened my eyes my vision was blurred but I could see the door was open. A sharp pain flashed through my skull, and whenever I moved little knives stabbed at my head. I felt gingerly about and my fingers brushed along the dried blood matting my hair. Using the wall as support and gritting my teeth, I staggered for the door, lurching like a drunkard. Little spots of colour danced across my vision. I reached the door, and grabbing the tarnished handle flung it open. I wished I hadn't. There stood the entire household, their backs facing me, all packed tightly together, heads bowed, their attention gripped by something in the corner.

"Hello?"

No reply or movement. I stepped up to the nearest one and reached for an arm. My hand passed straight through the elbow, drawing no reaction. I pushed forward; it was like walking through a cold breeze. I reached the front and all pain was driven from my head at the sight before me. Blood roared in my ears and pounded through my veins. Bella was chained in manacles, head hanging, blood trickling down her arm from cuts on her wrist. Her ankle was twitching slightly. Her body was bathed in the light emitting from the machine on the table. Charles lay on the floor, deathly still. The chest, still open, lay at his feet. The key to the chest and manacles lay beside him, its black ribbon inches from his hand. He must have fallen when he opened it. The locket also lay beside him, lying open. So, it had worked. I hurried to the machine and blew out the candle, angling the mirror away from Bella. I unlocked the manacles at her wrist and she fell forward onto me. I then unlocked her ankles and she collapsed, lifeless, like a rag doll. The manacles hit the wall with a clang that, in the silence, made me jump. I was too shocked to feel any emotion at seeing my sister like this, again. I didn't understand. I had taken all possible precautions to protect her. Blood still ran freely from her wounds and while my mind tried to process what I was seeing, I tore strips from my dress and took hold of Bella's hand to bandage them. The minute I touched her skin, her eyes fluttered open. The pupils contracted with alarm on seeing me.

"Ann! What are you doing here? This is your chance! Your chance to get away!"

A cold shiver ran down my spine as I remembered the last conversation I'd had with her, how I'd confided in her that I wanted someone to save me, to take me away from everything. She had taken it seriously, too seriously.

"Bella, what have you done?"

"What you wanted someone to do for you. What you would have done for me. Now leave and get out."

Her hand was holding mine so tightly that I felt a bone in my little finger click.

"You're coming with me." I heard a low chuckle behind me. "I'm afraid it's far too late for that now." I gasped and twirled around. I could now see the back of the room through them but I could still see their forms glaring and smirking at me. With a little twist of my heart, I recognized Lizzie standing near the front, grinning ghoulishly down at me and, with another little stab of pain I spotted Zac at the back of the group, his face twisted beyond recognition. While I watched, Tess drifted in through the half-open doorway and went to stand next to him, her eyes shining with a predatory gleam. In front of them stood Charles. His was the only body that still looked solid, but his form wavered and glowed around the edges.

"What do you mean?" I snarled. "What have you done to her?"

He looked mildly surprised. "Do you have no faith in my word, Ann? I promised I would leave her alone and I did. She has done this to herself. I simply showed her what to do."

"So, you have done something to her. How could you? Do you have no decency at all?" Behind me I felt Bella's hand relax slightly and I gripped it back all the more tightly. She wasn't getting away this time. She wasn't leaving this time.

"I personally have done absolutely nothing to her. Everything she has done, she has done herself. She thought you were in danger and indeed, you might have been had you not been sent to the village today. She thought that you needed saving," and he chuckled to himself. "That is the result," and he nodded to her motionless body.

"Well, I'm taking her away now. Keep your little experiments but she's leaving." I ignored Zac; he was a lost cause anyway. Bella wasn't. I was prepared to fight him, to do anything for her. But he nodded. When he waved his hand, the household parted down the middle, leaving my path to the door free. But he did smile a little at me, "Have you learnt nothing? She will not leave unscathed and neither will you."

"What are you talking about?" He didn't need to answer. At that moment, I felt the hand I was holding disappear, and in its place a cold breeze fanned my palm. My little sister floated up over me and across to join the ranks. I watched her go. I couldn't feel anything. I didn't know which emotion to feel first. Now I was alone, with not even Bella to stand by me. The ranks closed again, blocking my way to the door.

"But why?"

The sacrifice never turned. Hadn't I given blood enough time to know that? I wasn't talking to anyone but myself but Charles answered anyway, a look of sick triumph alive on his face.

"The light wants to change people. That is its purpose. When the chest had been opened and the light released, everyone in the house would be turned. I told you this. You might have been out of the zone but you were too caught up in the making of them to really escape. Your sister, however, had been hit by the light and survived. She was invincible against its power: the only one. Anyone else would have died. Being sisters you share the same blood. She gave her invincible blood, the only thing that could withstand the light to change all these people and, yes, it has saved you but she has changed."

Charles held his hand out to the ranks and a single figure rose up and stood next to him, taking his hand. I knew before I was introduced that this was Sara.

"I really should thank you, you know, Ann. Because, without your help, I would never have got my sister back." Sara was as tall as Charles and they had the same face, the same narrow eyes, and the same pointed nose. But her hair hung past her waist in scraggly rat tails and her eyes were flaming pools of madness. She was wearing a dress made out of the cloth ropes I had plaited from the dresses. Her dresses, I realised suddenly.

§

I was only half listening to him; the other side
of me was searching for a plan. I had to get out.
These things were ruthless and indifferent. Bella
was safe from them now but I wasn't. If I died, I'd
never have the opportunity to save her or anyone
else. Scanning the floor, I noticed the chest. A wild
plan started forming in my mind. I had nothing to
lose. I gauged the distance between myself and
the chest. It wouldn't take long but one false move
and my plan would be discovered. Charles was
still talking. I refused to look at him for fear my
intentions revealed themselves in my eyes. And
then, without warning, I lunged. Charles may have
appeared solid, but his hand evaporated as I fell
through him, reaching frantically for the chest. A
burning sensation shot up my arm as I touched him.
He anticipated my target moments before I seized it.
A furious scream rent the air and incoherent words
spat from his mouth. The ranks of the household
rose as one to attack, to stop me. But it was too late.
I hit the hard, wooden floor and felt my nose crack.
Stunned, the pain in the back of my head exploded.
Through the blanket of confusion dulling my senses
I heard a whistling sound, as if something was
headed fast toward me, and I rolled away seizing
the chest at the same time. I opened my eyes to see
what would happen. Suspended above me hung the
spirits, their teeth bared, snarling. I waited for smoke
to start seeping from their bodies, like I had seen
before. Charles was also frozen, his face contorted
with anger. I backed up against the wall, desperately
holding onto the chest; it was my only hope. Then,
something even stranger happened. Their bodies

elongated and stretched, drifting like smoke would, towards the chest. I watched them come closer, and vanish, every one of them, into the depths of the wooden box I held in front of me. As they vanished I felt a wind whipping the loose hair at the back of my head. The chest started to vibrate as it filled. I held it closer, securing it against me. Charles was the last to go in. I didn't look, but the minute he was inside I slammed the lid. Vibrations then shook my own body. I heard a clattering and clanging emitting from the box. Picking up the key from the floor, I rammed it in the lock and twisted it. I heard the bolt fall into place. Then I dropped the chest. The clattering and clanging still came from inside it. Like a weird crab, it started moving on the ground, shaking and shuddering. Odd yells and screams escaped at intervals. I looked for the knife on the floor. It was lying where Bella must have left it. Pricking my finger I let one drop of blood fall onto the lid. The moment it touched, it was absorbed into the greedy wood. I dropped the knife; it embedded itself in the ground, quivering. Silence filled the room.

Rose's Story

"Are we nearly there yet?" I asked, leaning forward
between the two chairs. Mum shook her head
irritably and turned the radio up another notch.
I sank back in my chair and looked outside. She
hadn't wanted to talk to me the whole journey,
instead turning up the radio until it blared out of the
windows. The scenery was a change from the dirty
tarmac and crowded streets but I didn't really see it.
Colts jumped skittishly and sheep grazed peacefully.
The air was alive with the sound of birds tweeting
and the rustling of wind in the bushes lining the
dusty track, but the only sound I could hear was
the music roaring from the radio. I wound down
the window and let the air blow into my face until
it felt cold and numb. The lane snaked along like a
meandering stream, and the pollen from the flowers
drifted on the breeze, in through the window.

A distant relative had bequeathed Fitz Hall to my
grandfather, but he had died in the winter. By rights,
it now belonged to us but there still had been a
lengthy court case in London. It was now nearing
the end of summer and Mum and I were going up
to see the old house. Dad would finish off the case
and come and join us. He'd had to sell his successful
business but there was another one, even richer, up
here and the thought of money lured my parents
like bees to honey. I wasn't proud of them and they
weren't impressed with me. Fitz Hall was an old
mansion in the north of England, as far from London
as I could possibly want; the nearest village was
two miles away. At first Dad had wanted to go by
himself but we'd won him over. It was far better

that we went first, to make the house habitable. I remembered that moment, sitting in silence. It was one of the few times Mum and I had been on the same side. Now we sat, listening to the radio, not speaking. When the house came into view I leaned forward to see it better. It had obviously once been a proud house. Now ivy grew wild up one side, its long tentacles stretching across the dusty windows. A few chimney pots had broken. No curtains hung at the windows. A weathervane, shaped like a cockerel, spun on the top of the house. It was very big though, they hadn't been lying about that. I tilted my head back for a better view as we approached it. Finally Mum turned off the radio and silence filled the car. She had to get out to open the large, wire topped gate, and then we trundled up the drive, white stones crunching under our tyres. Mum switched off the engine and its contented purr stopped. I opened the door slowly and stepped out onto the drive, hugging my rucksack to my chest. I revolved, taking in everything I could. The flower beds were a riot of colour, some weeds, some herbs and some flowers. Dandelions released feathery seeds that blew in clusters toward us and in the herb garden mint choked lavender and fennel as they wrestled for sunlight. I stared over the wall, looking at the untended fields, and then at the forest closing us all in. Mum dug around for the key and when she'd found it, an old rusty thing, she struggled to open the door.

The house had stood unopened for many months. There had been a funeral, then the estate had been sorted out and after that the court case in London. Because of the passage of time a musty smell greeted us but I didn't really notice. I stepped inside, feeling the cold stone floor through my shoes. My hand traced the top of the umbrella stand, shaped like the head of an eagle. There was a magnificent chandelier, all glass and crystal in tiers, like an upside-down wedding cake. The ceiling was covered in murals and paintings of angels and cherubs. It was very beautiful and I looked for some time. Mum picked up a vase lying on the table by the door and examined it, before replacing it. She pulled off her gloves and fanned her face while looking around. The floor radiated an icy aura which made me shiver. In front of us were two huge sweeping staircases that met at the top. Parallel to where we stood was a set of double doors, intricately carved and polished. "We should bring our things in first," Mum decided. I nodded, dropping my rucksack on the floor at the door. Most of our furniture and larger items were coming up in a lorry with Dad so it only took two trips to bring in all the suitcases containing essentials; stuff like clothing and cooking utensils. Mum left me, bustling off into the darkness. I stood alone in the entrance hall, listening to a fly buzzing by a window. Mounting the nearest staircase I trailed my hand over the banister. Through the double doors was another hall. Sunlight poured through the stained glass windows; the walls were covered with mirrors. I turned in a full circle, watching my many reflections imitate. The mirrors were all covered in a thick layer of grime but, in my mind's eyes, I could picture finely dressed ladies and gentlemen, spinning around and around to music played in the balcony above me. On the opposite side was another set of double doors: I pushed them open. Another corridor, full of doors that, when I tried them, were all locked.

Disappointed, I climbed another set of stairs to the next floor. It was more like a rabbit warren than a house. Stairs criss-crossed at odd angles and every door looked the same. At the top floor I stopped; there were only three doors, all old and peeling. The floor was covered in the same dusty, thin material. An insect was buzzing somewhere. I stepped forward; an ominous creak sounded under my shoe. The first door was locked, as were so many doors in this house. I moved back, stepped forward again and pushed on the next. The creak subsided into a moan; I took hold of the handle. I had expected it to be also locked but it turned quite easily, the door creaking loudly as it opened. Once inside I blinked. No junk or old cardboard boxes filled this room. Not a speck of dust or dirt on the windows or floor. A clean plastic sheet covered the floor. Sitting right in the centre of the sheet was a chest. It was a small, not very tall chest covered in carvings of animals and strange letters. I suppressed a shiver and approached it, drawn to yet repulsed by it at the same time. I reached the chest. Crouching down I looked. It had a big, old fashioned keyhole with a cover. I traced out a letter which looked a bit like an upturned flower pot Ω. Underneath it was inscribed the word 'Omega'. Saying the word over and over in my head I walked around the chest to the other side. Here was another sign, the letter A and the inscription 'Alpha'. I straightened up and tugged at the lid but couldn't open it. The lock was jammed. I kicked it; immediately I heard something hiss. Startled, I jumped and did a quick scan of the room. No mice. No rats. Nothing. Only the chest. I knelt down in front of it and put my eye to the keyhole. There was something moving. Definitely. I scrambled back with a cry. It triggered something because suddenly there was a scratching and scuttling all around the room. I leapt up and ran for the door. Slamming it behind me, my heart pounding, I realised there may be more secrets to this old house than I'd thought. It was clear the house had suffered much neglect and fallen to the ceaseless armies of dust, mould and mice. But it was also clear it had belonged to many generations, and all had left their mark however faint. Most belongings of the last inhabitant had been cleared out, but some belonging to the house originally remained. I found artefacts from across the world, all dirty but still fascinating. Swords hung on bedroom walls, and suits of armour glowered at me from the corners of the larger corridors. Shields, of every crest imaginable, adorned the halls and in one room I found a row of stuffed deer heads, their horns hung with cobwebs. Vases from China and India had been left, abandoned on various mahogany and cedar tables. There was a strong scent of artificial flowers in most rooms on the fourth floor. The attics bothered me but I tried driving them from my mind as I inhaled the scent of musty mysteries. Some floors had been swept, others left covered in dust. Bracelets and necklaces of every colour imaginable filled one of the cupboards, and in one huge third floor bedroom the closets held many floaty dresses that smelled of lavender. It was a site of bafflement but, right then, I was content just to wander, feast my eyes on each new thing and commit it to the right place in my mind. It was with regret that I heard Mum calling me at the end of the day.

Judging by the light streaming through the nearest window it was quite late, and judging by the sharp pangs in my stomach I had missed at least two

meals. With my head still reeling from all I had seen
I clattered down the stairs I felt sure would lead
me back to the front entrance. Not for the first time
was I wrong ... they didn't. Instead, I found myself
standing on another small landing but unlike the
others I had seen this had only one door. And it stood
ajar, as if someone had just slipped inside. That
prickling feeling I'd felt in the attic swept over me
again and the sensation of being watched intensified,
a feeling of déja vu, as if I was once again standing
in front of that chest. When Mum called again, I
made no move to answer; and I did not intend to.
My footsteps sounded too loud against the naked
boards and I shivered. It was not unlike those films
where tension builds and builds and builds and then
something jumps out at you. But this house was
deserted. Nothing could jump out at me. Except,
why did I feel as though eyes were drilling holes into
my back? The door opened smoothly. The first thing
I saw was indented marks in the wall; countless and
very deep; deep enough to see the bricks beneath the
thick layer of plaster. But they were stained a deep,
dark red; too rich for paint. I recoiled at the thought
of what else it could be. The next thing I noticed was
that this room was, maybe, the cleanest of all the
rooms I had been in so far. It was large and would
have been nice, if I didn't compare it to someone
dangerous and still. Three windows were set into the
walls, but from only two I could see out. The view
from one opened up onto stretched fields, all purple
and dark, and from the other could be seen the front
of the house with its unkempt flowerbeds. The third
faced away from the other two but was covered;
either painted or draped. I knew it was a window.
The last thing I saw was the bed. My immediate

thought was, 'if it had been a person, it would have been dead'. It was wrecked. The mattress was slashed open; stuffing spilled out onto the floor. The legs were all broken and cracked and the pillow beyond repair. On its remains lay something. I picked it up and looked at it. It was like a friendship bracelet but made of hair. Three different colours. One brown, one blond and one black. Mum called my name again.

"I'm coming!" I resumed my examination. It was very well and very carefully made. When I left the room I closed the door firmly behind me, feeling as if I was trapping something inside it. But, later on, when Mum asked which room I wanted, the words slipped off my tongue before I could catch them, against my better judgement, "The room on the third floor please."

§

"You left something in the car." A large book poked through the half-open door. I stepped up to take it, wading through my sea of belongings. It was the day after we'd arrived. Mum had thrown herself wholeheartedly into the hard, near impossible task of making the house habitable. That meant sorting out all the boxes, cleaning out the rooms and sending our marks into the very bones and foundations of the house, as countless people had done before us. I looked down at the book. It was old, leather-bound, large and very unfamiliar.

"Er … Mum, this isn't mine." I poked it back through the door. Nothing happened. She obviously didn't care what happened to the book; as long as it didn't haunt her. Typical Mum. I stepped over the boxes again and sat on my bed. The book was held shut by a big, old-fashioned clasp sunk into the old, cracked leather. There was no title on the front cover so when I opened it I read, 'A Timeless World' and there was no author.

"Why did Mum think this was mine," I muttered, flicking through the pages. It looked like a history book but, judging by the random words that jumped out at me, it was much more interesting. Thumbing through the pages, I picked out a paragraph and skimmed it.

'*The stories of Fitz Hall fill many of the neighbouring villagers with terror. Before life at the village had really flourished, in the time of the first Lord and Lady, there were rumours about horrible things going on inside the house. The Lady's first daughter, Sara, died mysteriously while out on a horse-ride. Her brother was not well known but everyone agreed he was a strange boy and it was believed he was obsessed with raising the soul of his sister. It is impossible that he succeeded but the rest of the family went missing one night, and the house stood deserted until the next generation came to live in it.*'

I stopped reading and turned the page. There was a picture of a painting of a pretty girl in her late teens on a fine, black horse. She was laughing and waving but I felt a thrill when I saw her name: Sara. What had the book said? She'd died on horse-back? Was this the same horse? Did her untimely death happen shortly after this picture was painted? I stared down at her again and dropped my gaze to the short inscription underneath:

'Sara Fitz (now deceased) on her 19th birthday. The horse was a birthday present from her father.'

I snapped the book shut then opened it again where it wanted, letting the pages fall gracefully. It landed on anther picture, this time of a sad-looking girl holding the head of another, crying in her lap. The inscription read,

"Anonymous artist. This painting was discovered, along with many others some time after the first Lord and Lady, by a young girl who worked at the house."

There were more by anonymous artists, all showing rather sad scenes; a girl crying in a dark room, a boy lying in a small stream with a large gash along his forehead and a mop of black hair, a blond-haired girl, and a black-haired girl comforting a little girl lying on a bed looking sick and ill. I felt a little unpleasant; a feeling you can get only if you are looking at a picture of someone you have known who is dead. Closing the book, I put it on my bookshelf between Jane Eyre and Black Beauty. I stared at it for a moment then turned to the task in hand. I could read it later, time permitting. I spent the rest of that morning arranging everything in my room just the way I wanted. This took a surprisingly long time, and when I finished I longed for fresh air. The house still had that musty unused smell. After telling Mum I was going to take a walk in the fields, I left the house via the front door and walked down the drive. The fields were reached by a long dirt track that wound its ways through a soft Paradise, filled with the gentle purples of heather and the hum of crickets. The sun had come out from its bed of feathery blankets and smiled happily on the world, drying the grass wet with the morning's rain. I walked for some time, weaving some flowers together just like my friend at school had shown me. It was then I noticed the ground rose quite sharply, and after running up the little hill I discovered a very steep slope. It too was lined with flowers, but at the bottom a powerful river crashed over rocks poking through its broken surface. On the other side was the beginning of a new forest, but further along I could see the remnants of an older one; of pine perhaps, or oak. Definitely something that cast big, dark shadows, with boughs thick and strong. I dragged my fingers through the grass, wishing I'd brought that book to read. My fingers caught hold of something; a chain of roses held together with ivy. The flowers were dead and brown but their scent lingered. I let them run through my fingers then lay it down beside me again. A rock dislodged and rolled down the side of the valley then disappeared. I followed its path, intrigued. When I reached the spot I saw, laid out in the side of the valley, the letters Z-A-N. They were laid with white stones and, judging by the moss growing on them, had been there for some time. I smiled down at it, imagining the circumstances in which they had been laid. Then I headed home and the letters faded from my mind.

As I'd predicted, Mum hadn't cared that I'd left and seemed not bothered I'd come back. Her mind was very much under the influence of the old house and how many paintings she could squeeze on the walls. I hadn't seen her the entire day. Passing the kitchen that morning I had seen the gleam of our new copper pots and pans, and there was already a pile of dented ones outside. Sighing, I headed to my room. It was very boring being an only child and sometimes overwhelmingly lonely. I picked up my childhood teddy bear, so worn and old it couldn't really be called a teddy bear anymore, and smoothed its ruffled fur. As I lay on my bed, I felt something hard and big under my spine, like a hard-back book. Mystified, I shifted to one side and pulled it out. It was the book Mum had given me. I'd put it on my bookshelf. Perplexed, I turned my head to look there and jumped. Between Jane Eyre and Black Beauty was a large gap, as if someone had taken it out, not wanted to disturb its neighbours. I picked up the book and went to the bookshelf. I slid my fist in between the books. The thing was, however much I stretched out my hand I couldn't feel the back of the bookshelf. Then I felt something rough scrape my knuckles and jerked my hand back. Then I realised, it was the bricks of the wall.

"But then, where's the back of the bookshelf?" I muttered to myself. Laying the book on the floor, I pulled out some of the others on the shelf and gasped. There was a very clear, very deliberate hole in the back. I ran my fingers down the side, while juggling some heavy volumes on one arm; I could feel newly carved wood and loose shavings. Feeling very unsettled, I replaced all the books and covered the hole. Then I returned to my bed and opened the leather-bound book. Instantly, I heard a hissing sound. I gave a frightened cry, something between a scream and a hiccup. Tucking the book under my arm, I carried out a methodical exploration of the room; looking behind curtains and shelves, moving cupboards and pulling out all the boxes under my bed. Nothing found. As an extra precaution

I checked on the ceiling, in case something was hanging onto the lamp.

"You're getting paranoid now," I told myself, but even so I took the book and my jumper and left the house again. Walking around the house I found, by the iron gate, a collection of old trees and a pile of chopped wood. I sat on the old tyre swing I'd found suspended from a crooked beech tree and opened my book again. It was early evening now and the old house cast large shadows my way. I rested my feet on the wood pile and delved into the world of the old Fitz Hall. As the evening aged, I learnt more and more about the house I was living in. The old mansion enjoyed a sinister history; each revelation more supernatural and ludicrous than the last. One thing was definite; the family that had first lived here, the Lord and Lady with their two children, did have a reputation which had haunted the house and scared villagers up till now. The son had tried to raise the dead, including his sister, but I couldn't find out whether or not he'd succeeded.

We sat at the newly scrubbed dining room table, eating the last part of our dinner: ice-cream. It was obvious this room had also had some work done to it, unlike the rest of the cobweb-draped house. All surfaces had been scrubbed to perfection; in the glass-fronted cabinets Mum's impressive stock of floral china boasted impeccable designs, and three of the pictures Mum had got from her mother hung on the wall. It was my parents' belief that the more pictures you had on the walls of your house, the wealthier you looked. I stabbed my spoon into the ice cream, earning a disapproving look from Mum. I ignored it, having had so many recently because I'd refused to help her sort out all her beloved pictures and paintings.

"Did you have an interesting day then?" she asked, wiping her tightly-folded lips with a napkin.

"If you don't want to talk to me, don't," I mumbled back.

"I'm sorry? I didn't quite hear that."

"Yes. My day was fine, thank you." I didn't mention the bookshelf. She wouldn't believe that I didn't do it. Putting down my spoon I took a large apple from the fruit bowl and bit into it.

"Are you looking forward to Dad coming up?" I shrugged. "A little, I guess." At least when he came there'd be someone else to talk to.

"That's good. You'll have to start school in the village as well at the end of the holidays." I nodded listlessly. I'd known that already. I hadn't regretted leaving school in London at all. It was a snooty school, full of girls who thought they were better than everyone else because they considered themselves prettier or richer. Yes, I was glad to leave it.

§

It rained that night. Heavily. Huge raindrops drove themselves in armies against the windows, lightning and thunder forked and rumbled across the sky. I stood against the window in storms and watched the heavens present a concert to the flash of white-bright electric light. I loved storms. I loved their wildness, their recklessness. I loved the lightning, so beautiful yet so dangerous and I loved the thunder, so loud and powerful. I opened the window and leaned out, enjoying the feel of the warm rain on the back of my head. I could hear the cosmic instruments wailing and howling, making the strange, ethereal noises and sounds. The dust was dampening and settling and the smell of wet earth filled the air. I looked at the fence. The shadows cast by the house and surrounding trees played across it. As I looked, one of the shadows began moving in a very strange way. I brushed the hair from my eyes and looked again, leaning on the outside windowsill to steady myself. In the light of the next lightning flash I was certain I saw a figure clinging to something on the wall, slowly shinning down a rope. I jumped back.

"Rose! What on earth are you doing? Come away from there immediately!"

"There's someone outside! Mum, look! There's someone outside!"

"No there isn't. You must be imagining things. Look at you all wet now, and you've let all the rain and cold wind in! Close the window and come away!"

There was no point arguing with her. Reluctantly, I closed the window and slid on all the locks, just in case.

"Pull the curtain!" I did so.

"Now look what you've done. On the wooden floor as well." I was indeed standing in a large puddle of water and my hair was soaked.

"But there really was something there. I saw someone climbing over the wall." Mum drew herself up to her very tall, impressive height.

"There is no one there, Rose. Stop messing about! I don't have time to listen to your stories."

I closed my mouth obediently. Mum cast her disapproving glare over the room.

"Look at this bookshelf. What have you been doing to it?"

"I was waiting to show you the hole there," I mumbled, pulling a dry T-shirt over my head. Mum turned her gaze swiftly to me.

"I hope you haven't been cutting holes in it. It's not cheap."

"It wasn't me!" I protested indignantly.

"Well, show me and we'll see what we can do about it when Dad gets here." I frowned, puzzled.

"But it's right in front of you. Look, there!"

Mum turned back to me. "Are you messing around again? I really don't have time to do this!"

"I'm not lying," I protested. "Look! Use your eyes!" I stepped forward and pointed. "Just there ..." but stopped. Where there'd been a hole before was now nothing. The back of the bookshelf was as good as new. I pressed my hand against the wood. It was smooth and strong. But that wasn't possible.

"No, there was something there. I promise."

"So, where is it now?"

"Maybe someone came and closed it up," I replied, half to myself and half to her. This made her angrier.

"That's ridiculous. No-one has been in this house for months and months. I don't have time to play games with you Rose. Now clear that mess up!" And she swept out of the room, leaving me staring agape after her. I never lie. Ever. I'd never really liked lying and I'd always followed the rules, so I'd never had to lie my way out of trouble anyway. Mum knew that. Why didn't she believe me? I knew I'd seen that hole, and I wasn't lying. I put my pillow over my head to drown out all sound. There had to be someone else in this house. I just knew it. I wasn't mad and I wasn't lying. The attics played on my mind. The more I thought about it, the more I was certain I was right. Someone had climbed over the wall, and I was certain that that person had cut a hole in my bookshelf and hissed at me. Why? I didn't know. Pulling out the torch I always kept under my pillow, I swept the beam over my room. Nothing. No one. I lay on my back and practiced making funny shadows on the walls; dogs, butterflies and tortoises. Suddenly I heard a scraping sound; loud and very much there. I dropped my torch and the room was thrown into darkness. As if on signal the thunder stopped its bursts of drum rolls, and all I could hear was the pounding of my heart and the ceaseless patter of rain on the roof. And the scraping. As if a saw was cutting wood - cutting wood. My bookshelf! There was something with me in the room.

I gripped my duvet and pulled it up over my head, willing it to go away, begging myself to wake up, if it really was a dream. The scraping continued, accompanied by a chattering that chilled me to the bones. It sounded like a squirrel, but squirrels don't cut bookshelves up. Then it stopped. There followed a grating sound, like something being dragged along a rough surface. I peeped out from under my duvet, shivering in fright. Lightning lit up my room. In the corner I saw a shadow ... of a tall boy or girl; a human but with weird contortions and too many arms and legs. I couldn't help it. I screamed. There was a scuttling and a scratching and a whispering all around me that sounded like it was coming from many voices. Still terrified, I threw myself at the light switch. My room was empty, untouched. Well, not quite. That book had gone and in its place was another hole. Now that I could see again my fear lessened somewhat so I slid out of bed and approached the bookshelf. I bent down and saw red eyes looking right back at me. I screamed. The light outside flashed on and Mum came in, looking extremely annoyed.

"Rose, what do you mean by ...?"

"There's something there!" I shrieked, pointing at the bookshelf.

"Now, not this again," huffed Mum. "If you carry on like this, you'll be in a lot of trouble!"

"I'm not!" I was so scared my throat closed, so that I could only pant. "Seriously, look. There's something there."

Mum rounded on me. "It's one in the morning! Stop this! I don't know what's got into you but I don't like this attitude! Ghosts don't exist! There's nothing in this house with us and your imagination has run away with you again. And I don't like this lying! Now, go to sleep and let me sleep too, you selfish girl!" She headed out. I was left staring at the swinging door.

It was only several days later that the unfairness and fright of the whole situation faded from my mind. I chased away the dark rooms and red eyes with bright light and warm sun. But a few cobwebs hung in my mind, kept there perhaps by both the facts that my book was still missing, and that Mum wouldn't let me forget. It was still another week before Dad was due to arrive but Mum apparently thought the situation so bad and I had behaved so outrageously that she phoned him and told him he'd better come up as soon as he could because I needed more disciplining. Not only did I have to listen to Mum's lectures everyday about the importance of telling the truth but Dad demanded to speak to me and I spent an unpleasant half an hour being yelled at from his office in London. So I retreated to the outside, away from the old house that scared me so much now and from the people that inhabited the house. I wandered about outside in a dazed trance, intoxicated by the new smells and sights around me. For the first couple of days I couldn't distinguish between them, so didn't know where to start imprinting them into my mind. Then, as I saw them more and more, I managed divide them into different groups and describe and relive them in my mind at will.

The forest was an ecosystem which had multiplied and reproduced unchecked and so unaccustomed to the presence of humans. There were the trees, the ugly oaks with their gnarled bark and lumpy trunks, the pines with their tall heads and purple and green needles that littered the ground. When I stepped on them, a bitter, musty scent was released into the air. And here the saplings, still struggling to find the sun and water they needed, succumbing to the ceaseless attack of other taller, stronger trees with their groping roots and spreading leaves. Twigs covered the ground in a twisted game played by themselves with me as the victim. The leaves overhead embraced each other and themselves so tightly that no sunlight found its way through, and so dappled gold-green spots chased each other over the rotting bark and dead leaves covering the ground. It was as if the forest was alive. I saw a deer, leaping away into the deeper undergrowth, and squirrels chattered at me, their tails things to behold. Insects hummed busily and in the muddy streams flowing sluggishly through the long grass toads croaked and gulped while tadpoles flicked through the shallow water, their gills pulsating.

It was a new world out there, one over which I had no control. The forest wasn't mine; the forest wasn't anyone's. No one owned them. These trunks had lived more years than mine and my parents combined. Maybe hundreds, maybe thousands. Trekking through that undergrowth, burrs and nettles constantly reminding me of their presence, it was not uncommon for me to feel like a stranger in this place. I saw hedgehogs, snuffling through the leaf litter for slugs and maggots, foxes with their sly red faces, and I once saw a badger lumbering off into his hole. Everything was exciting; everything was alive with that inviting danger. But I couldn't spend my whole life in there. Something came upon me sooner than I wanted. That thing was Annie.

§

School was not something I dreaded, quite the opposite in fact. Despite my bad experience in London I remained hopeful that this time might be better than the last. At least I could spend time away from my parents. Dad had joined us just before the end of the summer, bringing with him the many lorries and vans carrying everything from our old house including much he'd decided we couldn't do without, in the 'barbaric wilderness' as he now called it. I thought this to be a harsh and untrue statement about a place so beautiful and mysterious but I said nothing. They'd almost conquered the house now and all its fight seemed to be going out of it. The radio blared out from the kitchen everyday and I felt the mysterious silence the house had enjoyed for so long slowly disappearing. Dad's arrival also meant two of them to hide from. Whereas Mum didn't care about where I went or was as long as I wasn't getting in the way of her extremely busy and important life,

Dad wanted me within sight at all times, mostly so he could criticize me. School became an oasis for me.

The feeling of excitement was replaced by apprehension when I stepped into that form room, scared of what I would find. But they were normal girls, as far removed from the last lot as could possibly be. Most had the same sort of appearance, tall and bronze with elaborate hairstyles, but I was welcomed happily into their midst and I joined just as happily when I realised it was not because I lived in the largest, grandest house in the county. I didn't see Annie until the third or fourth week. She'd had to be there for the lessons but I hadn't seen her. But then, it seemed nobody did. She was the girl I'd feared I would perhaps become, the outsider, the one that didn't quite fit. She was everything I had been in my last school and she revelled in it. She shunned friendship, didn't want companionship. She was startlingly pretty but with a natural beauty that seemed to shine through, helped by her defiance and independence. She had black hair and startlingly white skin as if even the sun did not dare touch her. Anyone else like her would have used their attractiveness to become leader of the elite group in school, but not Annie. Because Annie was different. Different in every way.

We were in Maths, my worst subject. I was trying to conquer substitution, which hadn't worked for me before. Grinding my teeth over the impossible sums I felt a prickling at the back of my neck. I simply saw her. She was sitting at the back of the class, arms folded, only two desks away from me. I had a good view of her. The first thing I saw was a strand of black hair hanging over her cheek. She'd tucked the rest of her hair behind her ears but that strand hung down. If that was me it would infuriate me; that tickling you get when a piece of hair brushes your face like that. But she didn't move. Every cell of her body was still; she didn't even appear to be breathing. But, her eyes. At first sight they looked blue, but then I could have sworn they were green, then brown, then black. I couldn't make up my mind. They seemed to be every colour; both complicated and simple. I was transfixed by them, the radiant colours and the passionate feeling radiating from them, directed straight at me … it was pure hate. Flashes of puzzlement and mockery soured a wave of overwhelming bitter hate. She hated me. Her gaze bored into me, making holes in me, piercing through my skin and flesh and bones, making me bleed. Fire burned in them, a fire of hate that once might have smouldered but now blazed brightly. Unsettled, I turned around again but not before I'd caught a faint smile also directed at me, a smile of complete challenge, and a smile of utter victory. I was scared.

"Who is that girl?" I asked Rebecca quietly, discreetly pointing her out after the lesson. Rebecca snorted, "Her? Oh, don't even bother with her. She's called Annie and she's absolutely crazy. Her head is full of nonsense about the dead and raising them and all that. As a matter of fact, she's obsessed with old houses, yours in particular. Keeps doing essays on them for history. Yeah she's …" Rebecca whistled.

"Oh," I acknowledged. "Does she have many friends?"

"No. We tried making friends when she first came but she doesn't like anyone. She's not rude; she just doesn't speak when you talk to her."

"It's just that she was staring at me in Maths and I wondered..."

"Oh, she stares at everyone. She has a funny way of doing it as well. Like she can't see you but she's looking right through you. All the teachers love her because she's top of every class, even the pointless ones, like Maths." Rebecca hated Maths. She snorted and whistled again before saying, "Okay, see you tomorrow, yeah?"

"Yeah." I smiled. Annie left my mind.

The school was in the little village across the fields from Fitz Hill. It was about half-an-hour's drive away but the distance could be walked. Normally I did walk, because waiting for Mum or Dad to pick me up took too long. On one day though, I went to the village with Rebecca after school and so I rang Mum, who I knew was at the house, to drive down with the car. Fitz village was a nice village, quiet and, for the most part, deserted. Some parts were very modern but others were very old. Rebecca dragged me past the old church and down the main street that was really a hill toward the small charity shop. I had no idea what she wanted to buy so I went along cautiously. Hopefully it wasn't clothes or shoes. I hated that kind of shopping. But then again, knowing her, it probably was. The musty interior of the shop immediately reminded me of old museums and dusty exhibitions. The quiet tinkling of a bell admitted us. Rebecca's noisy chatter disturbed the silence; the young attendant looked up in alarm. The shopkeeper was nowhere in sight and I thanked heaven for small mercies. Rebecca, it turned out, was looking for a present for her mum, whose birthday was coming up soon. She went from item to item, giving a running commentary as she went along. I stood by the door, ready to dash at the first sign of trouble and gave an appropriate response whenever needed. It was with a sigh of relief that Rebecca, her newly purchased snow globe and I, stepped back outside.

"You're too loud," I said once the door had closed behind us.

"Nonsense," she laughed airily. "You're too quiet."

I sighed again. "Come on," I broke out all of a sudden. "Let's go and see the church."

"That's boring!" she groaned.

"Not to pray!" I rolled my eyes. "Just to see what it looks like."

Rebecca scoffed. "I wish you were a tiny bit more normal sometimes." But she came along anyway. The church was huge; a towering mass of stone and glass and wood held together with reverent prayer and penance. When Rebecca started to speak again, I shushed her. The silence was calm and regal; I didn't want to break it. There was a hunched figure kneeling in one of the side chambers but apart from that we were alone. I ran my hand over the many pews as I walked down the centre aisle, my feet taking the steps thousands had made before me. So many people this church had seen. So many secrets whispered to its deaf foundations. I stopped when I reached the altar. It was covered in a white cloth and purple flowers made a wreath around two lit candles. A crucifix stood in the very centre. I lifted my eyes to the gold leafed and intricately carved tabernacle and font behind the altar. Rebecca stood by my side for a moment and then walked away, looking at other things. I lingered for a moment longer and then left.

"Come on Rebecca," I called softly. "Let's go." I led

the way out of the side door and we found ourselves
in the graveyard that surrounded the back of the
church. I've always liked graveyards. I didn't know
what it was but I wasn't scared of them. I knew
the living were the ones capable of doing harm.
The dead couldn't do anything to me. Neither was
Rebecca, apparently. She went from gravestone to
gravestone, reading names and swinging her bag
from one hand. Her chatter was like an annoying
parrot. I followed more slowly, stepping carefully
around the neat borders in front of every stone, tuned
out to what Rebecca was babbling about. Then I
heard her calling my name.

"Rose! Rose! Honestly, where are you?"

"Sorry. What?"

"Isn't Fitz Hall where you live?"

"Yeah. Why?"

"Because, look." She was standing in front of a
grave. It was a weird looking grave and something
about it made the back of my neck tingle. The
cross was made of white stone. Leaning against
it was a crying angel. Another angel knelt before
the grave, also sobbing. I stared, a little unnerved
before turning my gaze on the words. They were
calligraphy and so took a couple of moments to
decipher the name I was staring at. SARA FITZ.
Something niggled at the back of my mind. I felt
sure I'd heard this name somewhere before and that I
should recognize it, but something didn't click.

"Yeah, that's the name of the house," I murmured.
Rebecca's voice bore down on me, breaking through
my thoughts. "Well, apparently she was only
nineteen when she died. That's sad. Maybe she lived
there or something. Or maybe her family built the
house so they named it after themselves."

"Yeah, maybe. Rebecca, we should go."

"Okay," she agreed. We turned. As we did, I caught sight of a figure on the low crumbling wall surrounding the graveyard. Annie. Watching us. I had a suspicion she'd been there a long time, just hiding from us. Looping my arm through Rebecca's I nudged her.

"Rebecca?"

"Mm?"

"Isn't that Annie?"

"Where?" and she looked round. "Oh yeah. I don't know why you're so bothered with her."

"Well, she looked like she hated me and I don't even know her."

"She hates everyone. It's just her way. She's weird."

"Yeah." We continued back to the school. Annie's eyes drilled holes in my back until we were out of sight.

In the car, Mum had turned the radio on, so besides the customary 'hello' we didn't have to talk. I wound down my window and looked at the countryside speeding past. My hair, caught by the wind, flapped about like some weird caged bird. "Come back into the car. Don't do that," came Mum's irritated voice from inside. We drove in silence for a few more minutes until Mum asked, "Who's that?" I craned my neck forward to see. A figure stood in the road waving its arms. It was holding something in its hand, a large book. As we drove towards it, it lifted the book like a peace offering. Mum slowed the car right down and stopped. I jumped when I recognized it. It was Annie. But we'd just left her at the graveyard, hadn't we? I leaned forward in my seat as Mum rolled down the window closest to her.

"Yes?"

"Hi. I'm Annie. You left this on your desk at school," and she handed the book back to me. Puzzled, I took it. When I saw which book it was I almost dropped it. It was 'the' book. The one that had been stolen from my room. By that thing. I gaped at Annie.

"Where was it?"

"On your desk. You must have left it there." A perfectly innocent comment; and her eyes were cool and blank, revealing nothing.

"But I didn't … how did you get there?" She didn't answer because at that moment, Mum spoke.

"Well, thank you but we must be getting on."

"Yes, of course." Annie pulled her head out of the car. We accelerated past her in a cloud of dust. Disconcerted, I placed the book beside me.

"Is she a friend?" asked Mum.

"Well, we're in the same form but we don't talk much."

"She seemed nice." I said nothing.

I returned the book to its place on the shelf. Then, on second thought, I took a spare blanket from under my mattress, wrapped the book in it tightly, and put it in the suitcase under my bed. I then zipped up the suitcase. This book wasn't mine. I didn't want it. And I was going to get rid of it at the first opportunity. Perhaps give it back to Annie. Rebecca had said she liked looking at old houses. Maybe that's what I would do, then maybe she wouldn't hate me so much. I fell back against on my pillow and stretched out my hand to rub the dents in the wall. I had washed out all the dried red in them and now could see the brickwork. I put my finger into one of them and wondered where they'd come from. Where had Annie come from? We'd left her at the graveyard and gone straight back to school; she couldn't have beaten us back. And she looked like she'd been waiting there for some time. How had she done it? Even if she had run all the way, we 'd have seen her arrive back at school, and that wasn't possible. There wasn't a shortcut; the village was surrounded by houses and halls. For some reason, thinking about it caused a nervous fluttering in my stomach. Reading about magic was one thing, but experiencing it was something very different. I shook myself. Magic didn't exist. I would just annoy my parents even more if I started on about that. I turned to face the bookshelf and then the wall again. I sat up and then lay back down again. Letting out a frustrated sigh I went to my table and opened the first book for homework.

The window looking out onto the fields still did not have a curtain; Mum hadn't found one yet; for this I was glad. I didn't like curtains but my parents insisted we have them despite living in the middle of nowhere. Putting down my pen, I went and stood by the window. Even from there you could see the fields were in a state; wild and overgrown with gorse and nettles and heather. I liked them better that way, but again my parents insisted they be turned into cultivated lands we could grow things on. Leaving my homework on my table I left the room, closing the door tightly behind me. Then I went outside. I walked to the valley. The woods encircled not only our house and land but also this valley. They didn't grow in a perfect circle, as I'd found out by walking through them. One side was slightly swollen so it looked as if the woods on the other side of the valley weren't part of them. But they were. It was strange knowing that whichever way you went, unless the forest let you pass through, you were trapped inside. I sat beside the white stones, the ones spelling out 'Zan' and picked up one of the pieces of gravel from the deep indent. It was jagged slightly on one end and not so white anymore; more like a brown or dirty grey. I gave it a clean on my T-shirt then put it back with the others. As I walked back, I suddenly remember where I had heard Sara Fitz from. It was one of the names in the book. So she was a real person. How much more of the book was actually real? And how much did Annie know?

§

The next day when I told Rebecca about what had happened, she gave the obvious answer. "Maybe that wasn't her we saw in the graveyard."

"But you were there. You saw that it was. You said so," I insisted, taking the necessary books out of my locker and shoving them into my bag. Rebecca closed hers and leant against it, looking thoughtful. "Yes but I didn't really look. I wanted to get home." I gaped at her.

"I don't like this and I don't like her." I slammed the locker door and stalked off down the corridor.

"Well no one does like her because she is so cold and she doesn't like anyone else because she probably thinks we're very stupid," soothed Rebecca, hurrying after me. "Just forget it. It probably wasn't her. And if the book bothers you so much, burn it or something. It's not difficult."

"Hmm," I said in reply, swinging my bag onto the table and falling down onto my seat. Rebecca was right. I could just burn the book. If it didn't belong to

Annie then I could just burn it. Get rid of it.

That afternoon, just as the last bell rang, I dashed
from the classroom and ran down the hall towards
Annie's locker. As I had hoped, she was there slowly
and carefully putting things back into it.
"Annie!" She turned slowly and her eyes widened
slightly as I skidded to a halt in front of her.
"Watch where you're going," she said quietly,
closing the locker door behind her. I nodded and
took a deep breath.
"Yeah, sorry. But anyway, I wanted to ask you about
that book I gave you." Her wavering attention was
caught again. Her eyes narrowed slightly and she
turned away from me, turning the key in the lock and
stowing the keys in her pocket.
"What about it?" she asked warily.
"Is it yours?" It sounded like a stupid question but
it seemed to make sense to Annie. She looked at
me, her eyes once again a blank mask. I swallowed
and slid my hands into my pockets to hide the fact
they were sweating with fear. I didn't like her. Not
one bit. Her mouth opened but then she raised her
eyebrows and seemed to be debating something
with herself. She closed her mouth and then opened
it again and said "No. It's not mine," adding, "if it
was I wouldn't give it to you, would I?" There it
was again. She made me feel like a stupid child. I
nodded. "Good," and then hurried to explain myself
because she was starting to lose interest and walk
away.
"I just wanted to know because I was going to burn
it you see." She froze. I pretended not to notice
and started to walk my own way, feeling as though
something heavy had just been lifted from my

shoulders.

"Rose."

I didn't stop walking, fighting the urge to run.

"Rose," she repeated, more urgently this time. I turned reluctantly. Annie's face was still unmoving but it had lost colour. I felt my heart quicken. That book did mean something to her. My mind whirred. Then why had she given it to me? Did it have something to do with that chest?

"Did you find something in it?" she asked, apparently throwing caution to the wings. I shook my head slowly, wondering what on earth she could mean. She closed her eyes briefly but I didn't miss it. Before I could press the matter however she asked, "Why do you want to burn it? Why not just keep it?"

"Well, I don't want to." There was no point telling her what had happened. If she already knew more than I thought then I didn't want her to think I was scared, but if she didn't know I didn't want to give her another window inside me when she already seemed to know so much.

"I think you should keep it." It could have been an order.

"But I don't want to."

"You have lots of space in your house for it. You have lots of bookshelves. Why can't you?"

"I ... how do you know we have lots of bookshelves?"

"You have a library. Everyone knows that." She said it so smoothly that I almost believed her. Almost.

"I've got to go," I stammered. I turned around and tried to walk away slowly. I didn't look back once but before I had turned around I was sure that I had seen her smile.

I slid the book off the shelf and turned it over and over in my hands. The faded gold letting on the front was peeling off and the worn leather was showing through. I skimmed my hand over the burnished brass clasp and ran it down the spine of the book thinking. I absent-mindedly flicked through it, not really paying attention to what I was looking at or what I was seeing. I had read it already. I didn't need it anymore and it wasn't helping anyone to keep it in the house. Flicking listlessly through the pages, I felt deep regret at having to burn it. It really was a beautiful book. But I didn't want it or anything to do with it. Let Annie keep her secrets but I had made up my mind; I didn't want to be a part of them. As I stood up, something fell from inside the book onto the floor. Stooping, I picked it up and turned it over. It was a letter but the name was on the back, not the front. It was my name. Rose. Written in the same script the book was written in. I stared down at the four letters, lying there so innocently and felt a great wave of nausea rise in my throat. It was my name. It was mine. The person who wrote the book left this letter for me. But it wasn't there before. It took all my self-control not to rip open the letter there and then. But I stopped myself. I couldn't. Anything like this was not to be trusted and I didn't trust it. I wanted nothing to do with it. My mind made up, I took an old rucksack from under my bed, put the book in it and on my way down to the door snatched the only box of matches we had in the house from the kitchen counter. Then I let myself out through the back, listening carefully for any signs of Mum approaching and hurried round to the front of the house. I went to the valley, my valley as I called it now. That was the most hidden place and my favourite. I struggled out of my rucksack, took the book out and laid it on the shallow rusty dish I had brought with me. I thought of the letter remorsefully and then shook my head angrily. No, it might have been addressed to another Rose and maybe it wasn't mine. As if it was…well, if it was I didn't want it. I didn't want it at all. Maybe this was proof. Proof that Annie did have something to do with it. Maybe this was another of her pranks on me. Well, this time I wasn't going to fall for it. I held the matches in my hands and looked down at the book. For someone like me, an ardent reader, this was blasphemous. But the book was wrong and it deserved it. A storm rumbled in the distance but right now the grass was dry and I didn't know when the rain would start falling. I struck a match and shoved it straight into the pages of the book before I could have the chance to change my mind. The flames caught surprisingly fast, bright and yellow and blue, leaping and crackling and in their wake I saw the book slowly turning into ash and charred metal and leather. The storm rumbled closer and I saw a flash of lighting fork down from the sky just over the forest. I turned back to the book. It was burning fast. It would be ash soon. I could come back tomorrow. Seizing my rucksack, I started to run back up the hill. Lightning cracked again, a jagged whip cutting cleanly through the grey clouds followed by a disheartened rumble of thunder. Rain started to fall, heavier and heavier, blurring my vision. At the top of the valley, I turned back quickly and saw the book still burning, the flames jumping higher and higher.

After burning the book, I slipped back into the house feeling much happier than I had in days. I let myself in through the kitchen, climbed the stairs and went to my room. Mum obviously hadn't heard me go out because no one was yelling for me in the house and so I wriggled out of my wet uniform and pulled on my favourite outfit. Humming merrily to myself, I jumped back onto my bed, pulled my diary out from under my pillow and, bracing myself on my elbows, started to write. My cheerful balloon was shattered almost immediately.

"Rose!" The irritated voice broke through my reverie and I felt the weight of gloom sink back on top of me.

"Yes?" She opened my door and asked impatiently, "Where's the key to the attics?"

"Hanging on its hook?"

"No. It's not there anymore. I wanted to take some of our pictures down from there. Have you left any doors unlocked recently? When you have been out?" I shook my head. She gave me another look and then left, still muttering angrily to herself. I shrugged, flipped back around and remembered something. I had been out. And I had left the door open. And I had the feeling the chest and the book were connected. Was this just another coincidence? Pushing my diary back under my pillow, I slid off my bed and opened the door, already calling to Mum.

"Mum! Mum!" She was on the phone. "Mum!" I shouted more urgently. She turned to me, while still talking and mouthed, "Not now!" I didn't care. I took the phone away from her, hanging up and starting to talk while all she could do was gape.

"Mum! When and where did you last see the key?""Really Rose! That's not a good enough reason."

"Here! Take the phone! Just tell me!"

"About two hours ago on its hook."

"Two hours ago on its hook, okay. Thanks."

"Rose? Where are you going?"

"Phone them back!" I replied, hurtling down the stairs toward the kitchen. All the keys were still there, apart from the attic one, just as Mum had said. I touched the hook, trying to pick up a clue. Nothing. I banged my head once against the wall. How could I have been so stupid? Mum was all the way upstairs, probably the whole time I was out. How easy could it have been for a young girl to slip into the house and take a key? But then, how did she know the way around? And how had she known we had lots of bookshelves? How did she know we had lots of books? She didn't strike me as a very honest person. No one else knew her so there was no one I could quiz on her character. And why was she so fascinated with my house? What if she had been wandering through our house at night? What if that had been her, cutting holes in the bookshelf and taking out my books? And why? Why did she hate me so much? Unless I asked her, I would never know. And she, with her smooth tongue and words, would be easily able to deny it. Leaning back against the wall, I thumped my head repeatedly against it, cursing the hopelessness of the whole situation. There was no such thing as magic.

Before sleeping that night, I locked my door and turned on my table lamp. That way nothing could surprise me. I then went to each of my windows, locking and bolting them. Feeling paranoia creeping in like a huge, black tsunami, I ran my hand along the whole wall, checking for weak places that could be used to break in. Then I took all the blankets that

I owned, wrapped myself in them and sank down into the protective, warm cocoon. The lamp shed golden light across the room and from here I could see the entire place, every inch. I was safe. I tried to make myself fall asleep by repeating that in my mind but then it became a mantra and distracted me. I couldn't fall asleep. Every time I almost slipped off into a light doze, something would move in the corner of my vision and I would jerk awake, yanking the lit torch I had in my hand from under the blankets, waving the light beam toward where I had seen the movement. I knew I was being silly but I told myself I just had to get through this night and then I would be fine. When it was completely dark outside I finally fell asleep.

I didn't know how long afterwards it was but dreams full of red eyes and creeping footsteps jolted me awake. Outside one of the windows, the one that had no curtain and had just been painted black, something slid off the roof and landed on the ground below with a soft chink. I waved the torch toward it but there was nothing. Nothing in here. Nothing out there. I was tempted to go and check the floor outside but I was too scared to leave my little defensive burrow. Wrapping myself more firmly in my blankets, I sat up against the wall. The flashing light on my alarm told me the sun would rise soon. All I had to do was wait. Knowing I wouldn't fall asleep again, I switched on my bedroom light. Nothing moved. I pinched myself and sat up straighter, biting my lip. There was no weird scuttling behind the wall, there was no strange movement anywhere. Everything was fine. I started to make shadow patterns on the wall, dogs and cats and butterflies and tortoises. They crawled up the wall and ran down it, twirled around in spirals and swooped up and down in zigzags. I wagged the dog's tail but instead the ears started moving; they bobbed up and down, like I wanted the tail to do. I dropped my hand but the shadow was still there, moving on the wall. I spun the torch around the room looking for the source of the shadow maker but there was no one there. The dog on the wall started to grow and grow, the ears moving eerily and then the tail wagging fiercely. I ducked my head into the blankets and begged morning to come quickly.

§

The next morning my head whirred and throbbed with a headache. But the thought of missing school and having to spend the day here instead made me feel even worse. I staggered upright and felt the world spin as blood rushed around my body. My alarm hadn't woke me up; a sleepless night had taken its toll about two hours ago and I had overslept. The sound of Mum rapping furiously at the locked door had woken me and so had a glimpse at my clock. I pulled my shoes on in the kitchen but as I did so, I heard something clatter on a floor upstairs. Mum was outside, bringing the car around to the front of the house. Dad had left. I was the only one here. Making a quick decision, I leapt for the stairs. Taking the steps three at a time, I ran to the attics. The door of the second was ajar. I felt my heart skip a beat. So someone had taken that key. Someone was up here. I was tempted to go and get Mum but the memory of the first two times this had happened stopped me. I would see Annie at school today. Her perfect mask had wavered when I mentioned the book, after all. Reaching out, I pushed

the door open with just the nails of my fingertips so
that I could see what was inside.

The chest had gone. In its place were four holes as
if the box had been ripped out of the floor. It was
nowhere to be seen but lying near the hole were four
dead birds. I looked at them in horror. Their plumage
was still soaked in blood and their beaks were open
and their bodies stiff. Mum's angry cry echoed
through the house and I was jolted once again by it
into a reality. I came down into the kitchen.
"Rose! Get into the car right now!"
"Mum, there's been an accident upstairs! I think
someone broke in!"
"Not this again! Rose, get in the car right now or
there will be consequences!"
"No Mum, seriously! You have to believe me!"
I saw, rather than felt her hand come down onto my
cheek. A sharp explosion of pain flared across my
cheek and fire blazed across my face.
"Get into the car now!" she yelled. "There is nothing
in this house! We are the only people here! Stop
messing around and get in the car this instant!" I
could only stand there, stupidly, holding my slapped
cheek in one hand. I had never before been hit. Mum
shoved me towards the car and in the process, I fell,
toppling over and jarring my spine on the ground.
My hand was grazed. Mum grabbed my arm and
dragged me upright. Opening the car, she deposited
me inside and started the ignition. She looked into
the mirror and glowered at me.
"You need to do as you are told!" she shrieked at me.
I sat still, gripping on to my seat with both hands.
My face stung but I made no move to hold it again.
"You need to just shut up and do as you are told, for

once!"

"Okay," I said in a low voice. Mum roared through the gates of the house and up the road. Dust billowed out around us but she kept her foot on the accelerator the whole way to school, swerving dangerously around the corners and slamming to a halt in the car park. I took my bag and rushed out of the car. I didn't say goodbye.

§

Annie wasn't in school that day. Alarm bells went off in my head from the first lesson when the teacher called her name and then marked her absent. I placed my palms flat on the table and tried to stop some of the jittery shaking that suddenly possessed my legs. The image of four dead birds was imprinted far too clearly on my mind and so was the growing shadow of a dog. When I picked up my pen to write, my hand trembled so much that my letters were all over the place. Rebecca looked at me with concern.

"What's the matter with you?" she said out of the corner of her mouth.

"I don't know," I responded, putting my pen down. "Have you seen Annie today?"

She shot me a strange look. "No. She's not in today."

"But she's always in."

"Yes but sometimes people get ill or have to go to things and they miss school." I gave up. She wasn't getting the point. I should have just burnt the book. I shouldn't have told her. And it had burnt. It was just a book. I blinked and saw once again the state of the attic. I wondered if the key had turned up. I wondered if Mum would go to the attics today. I wondered what she would see.

That day, Rebecca and I stayed at school in the library. This was partly because I didn't want Mum to pick me up. She was meant to today but I knew that she would only wait in the car park for about fifteen minutes and then presume I was making my own way home and drive back. It had become an unspoken rule between us and today it suited me fine. However, it was partly because Rebecca and I had a project to finish and the library was the best place to do it. I hammered away at the keyboard as Rebecca swung around in her wheelie chair and leant over the back of it.

"Rose? Why are you so worried about Annie?"

I stopped typing and then started again. I could be honest with Rebecca.

"I don't know," I sighed, logging into a computer and plugging in the battery cord. "I just think it's weird that of all the days she didn't come in, it was today."

"Well, what's so special about today?"

I thought for a moment and then shook my head.

"You wouldn't believe me if I told you." With a pang I was reminded of Mum's shouting that morning that still hung between us.

"Well, you won't know unless you tell me." That was true. But still.

"I just find her a bit too weird, that's all."

"Well, everyone finds her weird. She just is weird."

"But she knew that I had lots of bookshelves and she's never even been close to my house."

"Well, everyone knows you have a library," Rebecca smiled. "It's not a big leap of faith to say you have a lot of bookshelves. Plus there was that website put up about your house when all the legal things were going on in London."

"I knew that."

"And there were a few of the larger facilities mentioned, like the forest and the grounds and the library and things like that. It's a massive old house. People are interested in it. Annie is just one of the weirder ones that are interested in it." I had no reply to that. Stumped, I spun around and caught sight of the time display on the laptop.

"Rebecca. I have to go now. I'll finish this at home and print it off tomorrow or something."

"Okay. Give me that laptop. I'll start my bit." I handed over the laptop and opened my bag to put my pen away. My pencil case wasn't there. I remembered with a groan that I had left it upstairs in the classroom.

"What's the matter?"

"I've left my pencil case upstairs."

"Nasty," grinned Rebecca. We had the highest classroom; five double flights of stairs to reach it. But I needed it. Plus, I couldn't leave it here. Waving goodbye to Rebecca, I started my long trek back to the classroom. The door was still unlocked, thankfully, but the lights were off. The grey afternoon light cast a dim shadow on the twenty empty desks and chairs in the room. My pencil case was lying on the floor, under the desk. Bending down, I picked it up and stowed it away in my bag. While down on my hands and knees, I noticed something else lying underneath Annie's empty desk, two rows back. I wandered over and picked it up. It was another book and lying on top of it was a bundle of old pieces of paper. The paper was very thick and smelled musty. They were held together with a fraying black ribbon. Putting the book on Annie's table, I slid the ribbon down over the edge of the letters and opened it. All the pieces of paper were covered with black, curly handwriting. It was so oriental that I couldn't make out one word. Tying them back together, I put them down on the table and picked up the book. It was very similar to the one I had burned. It had a thick leather cover, a huge brass clasp keeping it shut and no author. This one didn't even have a title. I turned the pages but the book was empty. At least one hundred pages. All empty. Not even a mark or a smudge of ink or anything. All the pages were as blank and white as fresh snow. I ran my finger over one of the pages. It was smooth. It almost didn't feel like paper but like ivory.

"What are you doing?" came a sudden voice, and the lights flicked on. I dropped the book in fright. Annie stood there, in the doorway. She was wearing a long, red dress. Her hair looked windswept and covered her face. She wore no shoes or socks. And her eyes. Livid or furious didn't even begin to describe them. Even from here, I could see writhing, coiling emotions barely controlled behind her irises that flashed with all the colours I could imagine. The fires of hell would have chilled in sight of those eyes. I couldn't move. Paralysed, I could do nothing but watch as she started to rave again. "Nothing," I stammered. Her eyes flew to the book on the floor and the letters on the table. "Were you reading them? Did you read my letters?" she shouted wrathfully, snatching them off the desk. I shook my head, feeling my legs begin to tremble. "Liar! I left them under the table! I saw you reading the book!" I tried to reply but my mouth was suddenly very dry and I couldn't get out a single word.

"What are you doing here? Always sneaking around? Always thinking I'm up to something? Always spying! Who said you could read it? Who said you could look at it? No one!" She swooped down and picked the book up off the floor.

"Why did you come? Why did you come here? It's not your place! It was never your place! Why don't you go back to London, back to where you came from? No one wants you here! I don't want you here." I had the feeling that even though she was shouting directly at me, she was really talking to someone else.

"I'm sorry," I stuttered. "I had to come and find my pencil case and I saw them lying on the floor. I just wondered what they were."

"But you're always wondering what things are, aren't you? Always looking for an opportunity to make me feel bad, make me feel like I'm in the wrong when it is you! It is always you!"

"I don't know you and you don't know me! I'm never trying to do that!"

"I don't know you? I know you far better than you think!"Her face was very close to mine and I could see the pupils were glazed, as if she was really looking at someone else. Suddenly, the pupils cleared and she stepped back. She was breathing heavily and her hands were clenching and unclenching around the letters.

"Get out," she muttered.

"What?" I stammered, swallowing hard.

"Get out," she repeated. "I have nothing more to say to you." I swung my bag onto my shoulder and did as she said. At the end of the corridor, I turned back. She was standing in the middle of the classroom still, shoulders shaking.

§

It was raining when I left the school, very shaken. I didn't see Annie anywhere and, despite the fact I didn't really want to see Mum right then, I didn't want to walk home by myself. I took the journey half running, half jogging, glancing around every so often. The rain wasn't heavy but there was a cold wind blowing and my hands, holding two large folders, rapidly turned numb. I lowered my head against the rain and pulled up my hood but the muddy ground still sloshed around underfoot. With a sigh of relief, I let myself in and shook my hair dry. Standing next to the doorway were two suitcases and an umbrella. I eyed them curiously. What were they doing there? Moments later, I heard Mum's voice.

"Rose? Is that you?"

Mum came into view, walking very slowly and gracefully down the stairs.

"Yes," I said back stiffly. As if our argument this morning was still etched clearly on her conscience too, she didn't reprimand me for my lack of manners. I inclined my head towards the suitcases. "What are they doing there?"

Mum looked surprised. "We're going out tonight. There's a meeting in London and we're staying till tomorrow late morning. You've known about it for weeks."

"Have I?" I wondered, vaguely remembering being told but then it had slipped my mind in the wildness of everything else.

"All of us?" She looked even more surprised.

"No. Not you. You can stay here and work." I lowered my head. Of course they didn't want me with them.

"Right," I nodded, avoiding her gaze completely. "I

guess I'll just go and do some homework then." And I hurried up the parallel flight of stairs before she could say anything else. She had looked like there were a few more things on her mind. I slammed the door as hard as I could and flung the folders down on my bed. I didn't want to stay here alone. I wanted to go with them. As much as I hated my parents and Mum in particular right now, I would do anything to just sit in the car outside, away from this house. The silence that had been so comforting when not polluted by the sound of the radio or loud music now seemed expectant, as if waiting for something bad to happen. As I sat down on my chair, I could almost feel the eyes of the shadow dog glinting at me from the corner and hear the soft footfall of someone creeping around upstairs. Before coming here, I would have laughed but now I was scared that my paranoia was understandable. I would have told myself that Annie wasn't perfectly normal, wasn't human if I actually believed such a thing was possible. I was more than scared. I was petrified. I turned that phrase over and over in my head, wondering whether it had really taken that long for me to come to grips with it. She scared me. This house scared me. I just wanted to go back to London where everything was fine. I wanted to go back to the bustle and the chaos, to the noise and the blatant lack of privacy. I wanted to go where people could protect and hide me in their midst. Here I felt like I was standing on a pinnacle high above everyone, an easy target to prey on. I heard a faint tap at my door and ignored it, waiting for the sound of footsteps walking away. The tap, tap came again and I went to open it. Mum, who had changed into her long, salmon-pink dinner dress complete with a very elaborate hairstyle stood there, fist still raised as if to knock again.

"We're going now," she said, lowering her hand.

"Right."

"So, just do your homework and then go to bed. We should be back tomorrow near midday." I nodded again, my hand on the door ready to close it. Mum looked me up and down. "Will you need a new jumper soon?" pointing out the large tear that opened one of the arms. Even that sounded patronizing.

"If I need one, I'll go and get one," I replied coldly.

"Didn't you need to go?" Mum gave another small nod, looked down and walked away, her high heels rapping smartly against the wooden floor. I looked down the corridor at her retreating back and then turned around to face my room. The rain had lessened slightly but still ran miserably down the windows. I stared absent-mindedly out of the window through which could be seen the back of the house and then the forest beyond and blinked. Out of the corner of my vision, I could see a fast-moving speck coursing across the wet fields. If I concentrated on it, it disappeared but if I looked at something else, it was there, plain and clear. I heard the front door open and then close and, moments later, the rumble of the car's engine starting. I looked back through the window, sweeping the now deserted landscape for some sign of the speck. I caught a glimpse of it headed toward the valley before it disappeared.

Making up my mind, I scrambled out of my uniform, letting it drop, crumpled onto the floor and pulled on my jeans and the top I had been wearing yesterday. Seizing my raincoat from the floor and pulling on my shoes, I left the house, after grabbing the house keys from the dish where they lay by the door. The ground was muddy and squelched around my shoes at every step I took. The rain started and stopped but the wind blew constantly and the water from the trees in the forest blew over the fields and the house. I walked over the ridge that hid the valley and looked up and down its length. There was no one there. I slipped down the wet grass toward the metal dish where I had burned the book. The ash was a little wet heap now and the metal clasps, which had not burned were lying there, warped and half covered by grime. As I reached to pick them up, I felt a tingle on the back of my neck. I dropped the clasp and spun round. The wind howled in the distant forest and the rain quickened again. I was no longer alone. A little hunched figure crouched at the side of the river, poking at something in the water. "Hello?" I called but if the person had heard me, they made no move. I scuttled down the side toward them, sinking deeper into the mud at every step. "Excuse me?" I began again. "What are you doing ..?" I trailed away as they straightened and turned around. "Annie?" and my voice faltered and cracked. I tried again. "What are you doing here? How did you get here?"

She didn't reply. She just looked at me. Her appearance had completely changed from the one I had seen half an hour ago. Her eyes were huge and black and tears spilled freely from them, seeping out from the corners. Dirt streaked her face and tear tracks were visible running down it. Her red dress was soaked with muddy water and ripped around the bottom and her feet, still bare, were caked in mud. She turned her back on me and instead stared out across the river. Even in the dim light and falling rain, I could see her bare shoulders shaking. Lying beside her was the book, covered in mud and the letters floated around in the river in front of her. Apparently, it was these she had been reading.

"Annie?" and I stepped toward her. My foot sank into the mud and I looked down in disgust. The two of us were standing almost right in the middle of the river. Cold water flooded into my shoe and I shivered.

"Annie?" I repeated. She spun round so quickly I was taken by surprise. She pushed me hard and I staggered backwards, floundering and desperately trying to keep my balance.

"Just stay away from me! Couldn't you just do that?" she flung at me, her eyes blazing. She dropped back down to the floor and ran her hand through the river. But this time I didn't feel the cold thrill of fear as I looked at her but rather a hot rush of anger.

"Why do you hate me?" I cried back at her. "What have I done?" Annie stood up again, and I heard her breathing very heavily, her hair violently writhing around her head in the wind and her body quivering in her filthy red dress. Through the thin material, I saw her back muscles tighten. I swallowed but then clenched my teeth. I hadn't done anything to her; anything worthy of the hate she had given me. However, Annie stayed like that for only a few more moments before seemingly collapsing in on herself. Her hair hung limp around her ears and neck and the light was extinguished from her eyes, leaving behind blank, hollow, black holes. As she turned around, I jumped at the depth of sorrow in her eyes. Her beautiful features had crumpled and the tears ran in excess from her eyes.

"I don't hate you. I don't!" she repeated fervently as I snorted derisively. "You are a good person, a very good person, but the people I see in you are not. The people I see in you are cruel and I despise them."

"What do you mean?" Finally I was getting answers and, right now, I didn't think I wanted them.

"You remind me so much of people I used to know. They used to live there, in that house. I worked for them. I worked for him. And he stole my life away."

"No. You can't have done," taking a step back and shaking my head. "The last person to live there left about ten years ago and they didn't have anyone to help them." Annie gave me a little, sad smile. It was the most human thing I had seen her do in a long time and the effect was extraordinary. She looked like a little, abandoned child.

"I'm not talking about the last inhabitants. I'm talking about the first inhabitants. The people who built Fitz Hall."

"No. That's not possible. It was built hundreds of years ago. You're my age. You're …" Annie gave a short laugh. "Your age. I wish I was. No. I'm far older than you and your parents and your grandparents. I was here just after it was built and I worked for your cursed ancestors." Bitterness and loathing filled her voice. Her arms hung loosely by her side and she carried on speaking listlessly, all fighting power gone from her body.

"Everyone here thinks I live with my grandmother. Ha! I watched her grow and then went to live with her. No one knows, not even her. My parents died centuries ago."

"And she didn't question you going to stay with her?" I folded my arms. Annie looked up at me and then turned her gaze back down to her feet. "No. I can be very persuasive." Her hands were going into spasms at her sides, clenching and flexing and her jaw was tight. The cords of her neck stood out. Her eyes were still wet although her voice was steady. The enormity of what she was saying hit me all at once and I reeled back, away from her.

"You're more than one hundred years old?" I confirmed and Annie nodded. I stuttered in disbelief but not one coherent word made its way out. Mouth agape, I stared at the young girl in front of me. Then I clenched my jaw. "Stop messing around, Annie. That's not possible." A little voice in my head reminded me of the bookshelf and the attic and the shadow but I pushed it down. I was done messing around. Annie didn't react as I had expected.

"Do you want proof?" she asked tiredly, looking up at me. "I can prove it to you. I know it's hard to understand and accept but I'm telling the truth." There was nothing that I couldn't pity in her voice. I nodded. "Prove it," I challenged. And before I could react she had put one of her fingers on my forehead. The place where her finger touched my skin burnt and suddenly I was looking at her through different eyes or maybe she had changed. Her eye sockets were hollow and I could see right back into her empty skull. She was wearing scraps of clothing but the rest of her body was a skeleton. On one of her fingers she was wearing a ring and around her neck hung a garland of dead flowers. The finger on my forehead felt like skin though. I stumbled back, my hands to my mouth.

"Do you believe me now?" I nodded slowly, unable to take in what I had just seen. She was a girl and yet she was dead. The Annie I knew was back but I hadn't been dreaming. My burning forehead where her finger had touched told me that.

"It's a curse. We were all cursed. Everyone in that house. All because of him. It's our punishment. Our punishment forever. I was not in the house when the chest was opened and the evil inside released but I had been too closely involved in the making of them and therefore I could not pass unscathed. From that day to this, I have not aged in my body but in my years only."

"I don't understand," I broke in. "Where is everyone else?"

"Locked in a chest. I locked them all in a chest. Everyone." Her voice rang with horror at herself.

"How can you fit a person in a chest?" I asked stupidly, my mind reeling and my head swimming in denial. So there was something in that chest. I had seen something moving that first day in the house.

"They are not people. They are souls. Ghosts, you might say." I clapped my hand over my mouth.

"There are ghosts in my house? Lots of bad ghosts?" If Annie found anything I said amusing, she made no show. In fact I might have thought she was joking, that this was some great prank she had arranged had she not been crying and looking so defeated. I twisted my fingers together, trying to process this last piece of news. Then I asked another question that had been on my mind, "Why do you keep coming into our house? Did you take the book and make the shadow?"

"The book? My book, you mean?" Annie looked toward the metal plate where the ash lay.

"Your book? But you said it didn't belong to you."

"I wrote it, that's all." She shrugged. "I wanted to

record everything that happened, more for other people. I couldn't exactly forget myself. So I wrote the book. I had been living nearby here when I wrote it. I grew old in my normal life but the day I was meant to die, I simply lost all the time I had gained and came back as I am now. I travelled far but I could always sense them, trapped in their chest. I knew about a year ago that they were getting stronger, more powerful and so the house wasn't safe anymore. I was much further north than this place, waiting there when I found it out and so I moved back down here. Like I had expected, the house was empty. They are not so strong when there are a lot of living people in the house. I didn't know there was going to be another family moving in. There are stories in the village that the house is haunted. Of course, those rumours are closer to the truth than they think."

Her mouth twisted wryly. I could barely feel the rain anymore in front of the information I was receiving. She hadn't finished.

"I didn't know you were coming. And when you did and you discovered the chest, I knew I had to do everything in my power to get you out. I presume you touched it?" and when I gave a tiny nod she frowned in acknowledgement.

"They can sense living blood through the walls of their cage. You are related to one of them and that makes your blood all the more appetizing for them. They haven't been fed in years. They must be very hungry. The minute I felt them stirring, I tried scaring you in every way possible. I didn't know your parents wouldn't believe you. I put the book in your car so that you would read what you were getting into. I thought you would show your parents. I hoped you would show your parents. Then I let Imp in …"

I held up my hand hurriedly. "Imp?"

"Imp. He's a little sort of monkey creature but very clever and very mischievous. I sent him to take the book because that hadn't worked. But then I felt them getting stronger and stronger and I put a letter in the book, explaining everything. I gave it back to you but you didn't read it and then you burnt it." She cast another regretful look towards the pile of ashes and I felt a pang of guilt. "And so I thought I would try and scare you off once and for all. I made the shadow move and grow but I didn't know you had locked the door. Nothing worked." So the letter had been for me and it would have explained everything. "I found your letter," I told her. Annie looked up. "Then why didn't you read it? It was clearly addressed to you, wasn't it?"

I hung my head embarrassed. "I wanted nothing more to do with you. I was worried about what would be in the letter and I didn't want to do everything that you said anymore." We didn't say anything and then I remembered something. "So, did I imagine the hole in the bookcase or was it actually there? Anything I showed my parents went right back to how it was." Annie looked at me, not a little anxiously. "No, you did see it but then I put the piece of wood back. I thought that your parents would believe you. I didn't think they would say you were lying." Her story made sense however much I didn't want to admit it. I looked back at Annie and saw her looking at me hopefully, as if willing me to believe it. The rain had stopped and so had the wind;

everything seemed to be holding its breath, waiting for my answer.

"Please Rose? Charles took everything away from me, my sister, my only sister. He lied so much to me. I've been horrible to you but I couldn't help it. You look exactly the same."

"Charles?"

"The one who started it all. That was his name."

"Why didn't you just tell me, the first day you saw me?"

"I couldn't. I didn't want to believe they were back, I didn't want to believe I'd failed. I thought that if I scared you away, I was still doing my duty and protecting you but I didn't have to talk to you. I didn't want to talk to you. I knew I'd have said something bad." And she hung her head. I barely made the decision by myself. All I felt was my head jerk once forward briefly and then it felt as if something huge had suddenly flown away from where it had been resting on my shoulders. Annie smiled. "Thank you."

"What's that book for?" and I pointed at it, lying on the ground.

"This has all the names of those trapped in the chest written in it. It is simply another form of protection against them because I have taken it around with me. They are not so strong when parts of them are outside the house. That is why I was so angry when you touched it. It breaks the spell around the book. It is no use to me now."

"And the letters?"

She stiffened. "Did you read them?" A flash of the Annie I had seen in the classroom was back. I shook my head. "No, I couldn't understand them."

"They are letters that my parents wrote to each other

when they were young. I have travelled extensively in the time I have been alive and one of the things I did was to go back to where I was born."

"You weren't born in the house?"

"I came to work there when I was sixteen. My mother and father had died."

"I'm sorry."

"Don't be. They're happy where they are now." I nodded awkwardly.

"I should go back now. I will be missed," I muttered, pointing toward the house.

"But aren't your parents away?"

I stopped. "How did you know?"Annie gave another smile, a little secretive smile. "You forget that I'm at your house a lot more than you think I am and I have my ways." I nodded curtly. I still didn't like her, whatever she said or did. She scared me and I didn't trust her.

"Right." I started to walk back up the hill but Annie grabbed my arm. "I'm coming with you."

"I don't think my parents will allow it."

"It's not safe for you there and your parents don't know that I have been in your house an awful lot recently." She let go of my arm. "Please, Rose." Finally, I nodded, mostly out of fear. I had the feeling she was a lot more dangerous than she was letting on. I started walking again. Annie caught hold of my wrist. "It's cold and I know a quicker way back." I shook her off. I didn't like the feel of skin on mine that I knew was dead, even if it felt warm and strong. Her eyes glinted. I looked around, curious despite myself. "What? There isn't another way."

Her eyes glinted. "Take my hand." Pure inquisitiveness made me take that hand otherwise I wouldn't have. Immediately, I heard a whooshing sound behind me and the next second we were flying through the air so fast that the ground was simply a green and brown blur and everything else was blurred as well. We were moving so fast even the rain didn't soak us. I turned my head and the only thing not blurred was Annie who was standing upright, with her head back and her eyes closed. The wind behind me howled in my ears and the only thing keeping me upright was Annie's hand, holding mine in a vice like grip.

"Here we are," said her voice suddenly, very close to my ear. The scenery had un-blurred and I jumped when I recognised the surroundings. We were standing in front of the house.

"How did you do that?" I whispered. I didn't think Annie would hear me but she smiled back at me from where she was at the top of the steps.

"There are many things I can do now that I won't share with you. Yet." I pulled the keys out of my pocket and opened the door, stepping inside and closing the door behind Annie. She looked around in wonder.

"You know, I've never actually entered through that door. I can't believe that nothing has changed."

"Why have you never come through that door?"

"I always came through the servant's entrance and I couldn't find the key to the main doors when I came back." I put my keys in the dish carefully and then turned to face her. I still had questions.

"What about the chest?"

"What about it?"

"Where have you put it?"

Her face cleared. "It's in the attic, come on, I'll show you."

"I know the way to the attics, thank you," I replied primly.

"I mean, where have you put it now and where is the key?" Her face creased. "What do you mean? I haven't touched it." I bit my lip. My face was still tingling from the slap I'd received, the slap because I had seen something. I'd assumed it was Annie. But now?

"But it's gone. It was gone this morning. I checked. The floor was torn up and there were four dead birds in the room." Annie's face had slowly drained of blood as I spoke. I slowly trailed to a halt.

"What is it, Annie? What's the matter?"

She said nothing but bounded up the stairs, running as fast as she could towards the stairs that I knew led to the attics. Her feet left dirty marks on the carpet. On the fifth floor she stopped. She knew exactly what attic it was because she passed the first without a second glance. Extending her arm, she touched the door and it swung open at her touch, much more smoothly than it ever did with me. The door moved all the way back and even I couldn't help but see what was there. The chest was back, lying on its side, and the birds were gone.

§

"They're back," she whispered, her voice tight and tense.

"Who's back? What's happened? Tell me Annie." My breathing sped up, sweat broke out on my hands. The chest was empty, its sides looked clawed, as if by teeth and nails.

"They said they'd be back and now they are." Another shudder of fear rippled through me as

I heard her low monotone and saw her staring eyes. They looked resigned. I felt, rather than saw, something large sweep over my head. The next minute, I'd pulled Annie to the ground next to me as the large library book swooped back out of the room, smashing into the wall outside. I turned around slowly, dread coursing through my veins. I couldn't scream, couldn't shriek, couldn't breathe. What I was looking at was so impossible my brain wouldn't believe it. I saw the wall and the figures of people standing in front of it. Annie stiffened beside me, her breathing short and fast. My eyes roved slowly over them. A motley congregation of people; some tall, some short, some old, some young, all dressed in similar clothing, their eyes blazing with hidden fire. One of them stepped forward. A man. He was tall, with hair touching his broad shoulders. The air around him shimmered, the edges of his body were not defined, as were the others. His face was lit up with a repulsive triumph as he surveyed Annie. I felt her trembling against me, her arm pressed tightly against my own. The red dress dripped muddy water onto the clean floor and I watched it, out of the corner of my eye, run into the cracks in the wooden floorboards.

"Did you really think your little gypsy spells would keep me confined forever?" His voice filled not only the room, I also heard it inside my head, echoing in my brain.

"You were always so naïve; even now, you still have not learnt." He had no eyes for me and neither did Annie. It was as if they couldn't see me. I shook Annie, but to no avail. Her eyes remained fixed on him and her body shook, visibly. He was drifting closer and closer; all the while Annie shook more and more. Then his lips began moving but no sound came. Annie heard, though. She grabbed her head and sank to the floor, making no sound. I crouched down beside her, shaking her shoulder but she didn't notice me. She was mouthing words rapidly; the man only laughed loudly, lifting his hand as if to strike her.

"No!" I shouted, shoving Annie behind me, taking the force of his slap across my face instead. It was the strangest feeling. As if the line he'd struck suddenly blazed and froze at the same time. Something burning cold slashed across my cheek and I couldn't move, paralysed. Something screamed in my ear and I lashed out blindly, my hand colliding with something that felt as if I was moving it through honey or syrup. Then the crowd of them were gone, just like that. I stood there, breathing heavily when I heard a faint sound behind me and spun around. Annie still crouched against the wall but her head was lifted and she'd stopped shaking.

"Annie!" I rushed to her side, pulling her onto her feet. "What happened? Are you alright?"

"I'm fine now," but she leant on my arm, as if it was the only thing keeping her upright.

"But who was he? Who were they?"

"Charles, and that was the rest of the household. That was his grand army of the dead." Her voice was very bitter. "One I helped to create."

I said nothing but then tried, "That … was Charles?"

"Yes," she said softly, looking at the floor. "Judge me if you want to Rose. I still hate myself for ever falling into his grip." I brushed aside her comment. "That doesn't matter. Where are they now?"

"Gone, but they'll be back. Charles can't touch someone living, like you, and stay in their presence.

He and his army will have gone to recover. He is their life force and they are his. If he dies, they go back to how they were, but he will live even if only one is standing. It was his ultimate protection."

"I see. And how do we get rid of him?" Annie let go of my arm and hobbled toward the opposite wall, trying out her legs. She shrugged. "I don't know." She refused to meet my gaze.

"You're lying. Why are you lying?" She didn't reply. I felt a surge of anger again.

"Annie ..."

"What?" she snapped. "Exactly what?" Desperation replaced my anger. For some reason, she didn't want to tell me, but she knew.

"I know you know. Why don't you want to get rid of them?" Annie still refused to look at me or to answer. I sighed with frustration and stamped my foot.

"Please." I hated that I was begging. I shouldn't have to be begging. When she spoke, she spoke so softly I didn't catch her first words.

"I don't want to not see them again," she murmured, leaning against the wall.

"Them?"

"Bella," she whispered, "and Zac."

"Who are they?"

She didn't reply for so long I thought she wasn't going to. I opened my mouth to repeat the question but then she murmured.

"My little sister and my best friend. The only way I can see them again is if I leave them here. I've missed them for so long. I don't want to give them up." I gaped at her.

"Annie, they aren't who they were before. They've changed." She whirled around, fists clenched.

"They haven't changed. They are still who they were before. It's he who's changed. No one else." But her voice caught and I could tell she didn't believe it herself. I pressed on, ignoring the uncomfortable feeling of bullying as I did.

"Annie, they have. You know they have. And he hasn't changed. He probably was always like that." Confusion clouded her gaze; and I felt I was onto something. Finally, she shook her head. "I can't remember. I know I should remember something but every time I almost catch it, it slips away again. All I can remember is that he wasn't always like that. He cared ... once upon a time."

I barely suppressed a scream of exasperation. He'd done something to her, must've done. Not half an hour before, she'd hated him with all her soul. Now what had happened? Time was ticking by and the ominous silence and open chest a constant reminder we weren't alone in this house.

"Annie, I know you want your sister back, and your friend. There are things I want too." I thought of my parents and that morning and it took a moment to force down the lump blocking my next words, "But it won't help. They've changed, and he's tricked you into thinking like this. About half an hour ago, you hated him. Remember?" She wouldn't look at me. "How do we get rid of them? Please Annie." She looked up and I saw new resolve break over her tear-stained face. She slid her hand into the pocket of her dress and I saw her clench something.

"Come on then. I'll show you."

We stopped outside my room. "In here?" I asked. She nodded, pushing open the door.

"This used to be his study," she explained. "We need

something from here." She picked up a textbook lying on the floor and approached the wall. I watched her, bemused, while she scrutinized every inch on it, running her hand over the whitewashed surface. Then a faint grin quirked her mouth and, raising the textbook, she brought it down with all the force she had against the wall. A faint crack, a pause, and the whole wall crumbled down. I clapped my hands to my mouth. A billow of dust filled the air and hid her from view for a moment, but when it settled there wasn't a speck on her. Where the wall had been was now an old door with a very rusty handle. Annie felt in her pocket and drew out a key. Shoving it into the keyhole, she wrenched it around; with a squeak, it yielded. I took a step forward. "How did you know that was there?" I asked, trying to steady my voice.

"Because I put it there," she replied, before opening the door and entering. Not wanting to be left behind, I stepped forward, picking my way through the dust and broken bits of plaster. The room was swathed in cobwebs and something crunched under my feet. I couldn't see for the dust swirling in the air. Annie was moving around further into the room. I squinted, covering my mouth and nose. There was the flare of a match and a hissing sound then the dust slowly disappeared. I saw the room properly. I gasped. Piled up to the ceiling, covering all the walls was a mountain of treasure. I turned full circle, mouth agape. Gold necklaces and bracelets piled high, medallions in tarnished silver and dirty bronze hung from hooks on the ceiling. Emeralds, rubies, sapphires, bigger than my two fists put together gleamed dully under a layer of dust. There were piles, heaps of gold and silver coins. Three suits of armour, in pieces, stood in a corner. On the other side were swords and bows and shields and helmets, all covered in dirt, but very much still there. In the middle of the room stood a table, but Annie was standing in front of it so I couldn't see what was there. There were no windows. Instead the walls were covered in carvings and strange hieroglyphics. Spluttering lamps were positioned around the room, lighting it up.

"Like it?" Annie asked, fiddling with something on the table.

"How did you get all this?"

"You forget, I've been alive much longer than you. I had lots of time to collect things plus, I took all the things from the treasury and put them here," she smiled, lighting something and standing back. The light that Annie had been blocking hit me in the face and I looked away.

"What is that?"

"This is what was used, to make them like that," Annie said quietly. I moved out of the glare of the light and saw the thing properly. It was long, oblong with a winch on one side and a piece of material on the other. There was a lit candle standing upright under a piece of glass and a beam of golden light, magnified from the candle, lit the room. I looked with some disbelief.

"That little thing?" I scoffed. Annie jerked her head up. "Yes," she affirmed. "This little thing. Don't underestimate what you see." There was a sudden clatter from downstairs and I jumped.

"What was that?"

"We're not alone here," she reminded me. Stepping forward into the light, she bent her head to examine it again.

"So how do we use it?" I asked with some trepidation.

"We must find his bones," she murmured, lifting her head at last.

"His bones?"

"Yes. We needed something alive to make them dead so we'll need something dead to make them alive."

"But we don't want them to be alive," I contradicted with some panic. Annie looked up at me, faintly amused. "Don't worry. The minute they are alive, they will turn to dust. They were all meant to have died years and years ago." I nodded. The plan had gaping holes in my opinion, but Annie was the expert and she seemed to think it would work.

"Why just his bones?"

"They're all tied to him. If he goes, they all go." I nodded again.

"I see. How do we find them?"

"They're here, in this room."

I jumped and spun around. "Where?" She jerked her head towards one of the suits of armour. I took a step away from it.

"Why?" I asked, weakly.

"I knew that one day they'd come back," she replied matter-of-factly, striding towards the nearest one. "Don't worry. It's only a skeleton. This bit of him is definitely dead."

I turned my head away as she raised the visor. A few seconds later I heard a sickening crack then heard her walking back to the table. She didn't seem in the least bit shaken. I refused to look at the section of bone in her hand and was very relieved when she slid it into the machine. She then stood back and watched. The candle slowly dimmed then went out. In the light of the lamps, I saw Annie's expression slowly morph into a mask, her face slowly hardening and hardening, surrounded by a frame of matted black hair. Her teeth clenched. But the light shining from the mirror just changed colour, lightening until it was a pearly white. Annie gasped.

"It worked," she said simply.

"So, they're gone?" I inquired. Annie said nothing, just looked at the machine and the light, putting her hand through the pearly whiteness and prodding the machine. Then she stiffened.

"Oh no, they're not gone yet. Come on," Grabbing my hand, she ran through my room and out into the corridor. Once outside I heard a strange whistling, like a steam train but, from a very long distance away.

"What is that?" I shouted, as we ran towards the front door.

"Just keep running," Annie ordered. I detected a subtle undertone of barely contained panic. We hurried towards the main staircase. Beyond that was the door. The whistling was growing louder and louder but I couldn't see where it was coming from. Before we got there, Annie yanked us both down to the floor. Before I could ask, several large vases came flying out of nowhere and smashed on the wall. Annie didn't stop. Pulling us up, we clattered down the staircase and sprinted for the door. We both tugged at the handles. They wouldn't budge. It had been locked from the outside. Annie looked around wildly, maybe searching for something to break the lock with, but there was nothing.

"Duck!" A large tome smashed into the door.

"Annie, what's happen ..?"

I didn't get to finish. At that moment, the two double

doors blew inwards. Annie just had time to fasten her hand on my wrist before we were both blown backwards, tumbling like rag dolls, up and over the top banister. I crashed to the floor, pain shot up my back. Dazed, I dimly registered the sound of footsteps leisurely climbing the stairs. Where was Annie? I caught hold of something that stirred and tightened my grip, using the now broken banister to pull myself upright. Swimming in and out of focus a pair of shiny leather boots stopped in front of me. My head was throbbing and I couldn't see what was going on. There was a loud crack and a little cry of pain. I knew what was happening. I'd felt it just that morning. I felt a stirring of rage from somewhere deep inside me. It wasn't fair. Nothing was fair. With one final effort, I threw myself over Annie in a last ditch attempt to protect her from the hand that was falling again. I braced myself for the stab of pain I knew must be coming. But it never did. There was a loud chattering from somewhere and something landed on my shoulder. Claws dug loosely into the top of my arm and hissed. My vision slowly returned and I squinted, trying to see what it was. There was a curse, and the weight went from my shoulder and then another hiss. The man standing there was batting at something clawing at his face; a little black monkey-like creature with an inky blue, long barbed tail. He turned momentarily and I recognized the red eyes. It was the little creature Annie had spoken of. Annie! I snapped my attention back to her. Her hair was even more dishevelled and blood ran from a cut on her forehead. One strap of the red dress had slipped down and the skin of her neck was even whiter that the skin of her face.

"Annie!" I shouted, shaking her. Her eyes opened

slowly, taking a moment to focus.

"Come on!" I urged. "We have to move! Now!"
The little monkey was still clinging onto his face;
we scrambled around under the fight. Pushing our
way through the double doors we entered the hall. I
locked them behind us.

"What happened? What went wrong?" I demanded.
Annie said nothing, simply seized my arm and
dragging me towards the other end.

"Annie?" She continued walking but started firing
things back at me. "They're not quite alive yet.
They're just a lot stronger. We need the direct light."
She pulled me to the end of the hall and we exited
through there. We'd barely made it two paces before
I heard it ... Annie too.

"Coward," it whispered; a low voice echoing
through the corridor we were standing in. I turned
to Annie but her eyes had gone strangely glazed
and she started moving towards the voice as if in a
trance.

"Annie! Annie, stop!" I pulled on her arm but
in vain. She simply shook me off. Seeing no
alternative, I followed her as she paced down the
carpeted floor, drawn towards the voice like a moth
to a flame. We entered one of the rooms on the
edge. It was small and dusty and inside was only a
painting of a small boy on horseback. Annie gave it a
hard stare before looking around. Her eyes were still
glazed.

"Coward," came the voice again, this time from
overhead. I looked up and screamed. Hanging from
the broken, dusty chandelier was the boy and girl I'd
seen earlier, standing in the group of ghosts, grinning
maliciously down at us.

"Coward," they hissed, but although their mouths

moved their voices came from everywhere.

"I'm sorry," Annie whispered. "I never wanted either of you to go. I tried."

"Did you?" jeered the girl. She didn't look any older than ten but her face was cruel and old, her mouth twisted. "So you tried to tell me what you were doing? You tried to stop me did you? You could have stopped me, if you'd wanted to."

"If you had wanted to," echoed the boy, dangling from his feet from the light, "you didn't have to help him. If you had wanted to, you could have stopped it. You had the power." I stared at them in horror. They hadn't noticed me. Annie was mesmerised by them. Whenever they were around, she succumbed to their power totally and utterly. But it hadn't affected me, yet. Looking round, I seized a large book from the lopsided mantelpiece and chucked it. It flew straight through the pair of them but they reacted sharply, staring around and hissing in pain. I made to throw another but something grabbed my arm, twisting it hard so the book fell from my hand. Annie.

"Don't hurt them!" I stared at her in shock. Her eyes glowed red and her teeth were bared in a snarl.

"Annie?"

"Don't hurt them, I said! Leave them alone!" Behind her, I saw the two of them laughing, taunting.

"No, Annie! Move!" I pushed her out of the way, stumbling over to the book.

"Rose! Leave them alone!" I ignored her and threw the book again. The little girl recoiled, losing her balance, falling to the ground. Instead of hitting it, she flew against the ground, swooping back up to hiss at me, catching my shoulder so that I fell to the ground and, unlike her, I hit it hard. She hissed again, the sneer looking so wrong on her little face. Out of the corner of my eye I saw Annie watching the whole scene in a sort of transfixed mixture of fascination and horror.

"Annie!" I shouted but she didn't hear me. The boy was still cackling madly, swinging from the chandelier. The girl held me to the ground, probing the skin above my heart cautiously, as if she was testing out an idea. Then her eyes flared with excitement and I began to feel peculiarly woozy, the kind of feeling you get if you drink a lot of alcohol very quickly.

"Annie!" I shouted again but my voice sounded weak and fluttery. This, if nothing else, startled her out of her reverie.

"Bella! Get away from her!" She ran at the girl, waving her arms. It would have looked funny if the situation hadn't been as far removed from funny as could be. Annie pulled me to my feet. Bella shrank back from us, her mouth tinged with a dark liquid. Was that my blood? Was that what she'd been doing?

"But she tastes so good and I'm so hungry," she purred, licking her lips. I shuddered as I saw her teeth were similarly stained. Annie shook her head sadly, keeping herself between me and her parasitic sister.

"Bella, what happened to you?" The girl on the floor thrashed about, but the boy hanging from the chandelier froze when he heard Annie's voice. I tried to peer around her but Annie was stronger than me, and my head was throbbing.

"It's your fault! It's your fault!" Bella charged accusingly. "Without you, I wouldn't be like this!

Without you, I would be dead!"

"I never meant for you to be like that! You chose to go to him! If you'd asked me, I'd have never let you go! You chose a day when I wasn't there! You didn't do as I said! I never wanted you to be like that!" The boy had joined in, chanting the words but mingling them with hisses and sneers.

"You chose to help him. Without you, he'd never have succeeded. Without you, I would not be like this. I warned you to not give in to him but you did!"

"I gave in because I was worried for my sister! I was worried for all of you!"

"Liar!" Their voices echoed around the room. I pressed myself against the wall and watched the exchange going on in front of me. Annie's back was straight and strong, her face sad but resolved. These two could not affect her like Charles could.

"I'm not lying! I saw what he did! And I was terrified for the pair of you. For you Bella, my only sister and you Zac, my best friend. Have you forgotten everything from that time? Have you forgotten how you told me you didn't blame me, how you said you'd do the same thing if you were in my place?"

I watched in awe as Annie's body started glowing. I had to avert my eyes. Her voice rippled with pent-up emotion.

"I never wanted this for either of you. I never wanted you to be trapped that way. But I have not escaped. I have lived every minute of these hundreds of years like you, with you. I am no different."

"You've been alive," Zac snarled. Annie tossed her hair angrily.

"And I should have died years ago. I've felt the same

pain as you both have. And now I will try and end it, if I can." She flicked her hands and the air around her figure seemed to explode in a sudden release of energy. Zac and Bella were blown backwards against the wall. Annie helped me up and together we left the room. Once out the room Annie braced a hand against the wall for support.

"I shouldn't have done that," she muttered ruefully. "I lost my temper."

"Temper is never attractive," I murmured back.

"That's what my mum says," I explained hastily as Annie's head shot up and her eyes narrowed.

"Indeed," and she raised her eyebrows.

"Annie, what do we do?" I asked urgently. Even though she seemed to have two of them under control there were many left.

"We need to go and get the machine. Only then can we really destroy him." We retraced our steps back to my room. He was already there. As if waiting for us.

§

He was facing away from us, looking at the machine on the table with great interest. The light had gone out. We'd made no noise when we went in, yet it was as if he knew we were there, and was playing with us. I felt Annie stiffen up beside me and put my hand on her arm. She looked at me and smiled a faint tense smile. It reminded me of the eye of the storm.

"Charles." He took his time turning around. His face still bore scratches from his fight with Imp.

"Ann. So nice of you to appear. I was about to go and find you myself. And I see you've brought a little friend with you." It was the first time he'd actually acknowledged my presence and I felt a sputter of fear at the way he'd said 'little friend.'

"I'm impressed at what you've done. Maybe you were listening to me after all."

"Of course I listened," Annie snapped. "I listened to all your lies."

"My lies?" He raised his eyebrows. "And yet here we both stand, hundreds of years after we were meant to die, still living and breathing. I didn't lie about everything. Be truthful Ann, and tell me you are at least a tiny bit impressed."

"I'm not impressed," she denied. "I'm disgusted at the lengths you went to get here."

"Were wars ever won without the loss of lives?" he countered. "I made the sacrifices I had to. But I still stand, the greatest and most powerful man in the world."

"A world that does not know of your success," Annie mocked. I shot her a quick glance. This wasn't the time to lose her temper. He could easily crush us both. Annie may have had some power but it was miniscule compared to his. His voracious vitality and predatory nature simmered in the air like an approaching storm. And I had nothing against the pair of them.

"Not yet," he smiled. "But your friend is part of that world, is she not?"

"She is nothing with this. You will leave her be."

He smiled. "As you wish, Ann, as you wish." The minute he'd said that, the two of them reacted almost simultaneously. Annie pushed me away from her with more strength than I'd ever have believed she possessed, and Charles flew at the pair of us. Annie spun round a fraction of a second too late and Charles caught her by the neck, throwing her against the wall, pinning her there. He flicked his hand, making a very similar motion to the one Annie had made in the room, and a blast of air flung me against the wall. I heard Annie scream my name. The impact winded me and I sat there, gasping like a fish, curled up around myself before I could summon the strength to straighten myself. A horrible gagging sound brought me to my senses and I twisted, ignoring the consequential tipping feeling in my head. Annie's face was turning bluer and bluer under the constriction of her windpipe. She was clawing at the hand was holding her there, slightly suspended off the ground, but to no avail.

"Rose!" she wheezed. "Light the candle! Light the candle!"

Charles turned to face me, his hand still slowly strangling Annie. She was shaking her head, trying to throw him off but her movements were becoming weaker and weaker. Charles raised his eyebrows at me. When he spoke, his lips moved but his voice reverberated in my head, quietly and softly. It could have belonged to someone other than the person who, at present, was throttling a girl against the wall. "Really? Is that really the right thing to do?" He held out his free hand towards me.

"You're fighting a losing battle and you will lose. Don't listen to her Rose, listen to me." Through the intoxicating sound of his voice in my head, I heard another one, a desperate, choking one.

"He's lying to you! Don't listen to him, Rose! He can't kill me! Turn on the light! Kill him!" Charles seemed oblivious to the cries behind him. He chortled quietly. "This isn't your fight, Rose. What would your parents say if they found you doing this? Would they be happy? Isn't that what

you want, to make them happy?" I was trapped. By
his words. Under the magic I could taste in the air,
against my tongue. It was what I wanted, to make
them happy. For them to be happy with me, with
the daughter they'd been given. I didn't want them
to keep imagining and fantasising about what might
have happened. I could feel my head nodding, even
though I myself was making no move to do so.
"You share my blood, Rose, and I have done
extraordinary things. You can do them too if you
want. And I'll help you. Think of your parents."
"No Rose! Don't listen to him! He's lying! Kill him!
Kill him now!"
"You need to make a choice. You know what the
right one is. Just say it Rose." There was fogginess
in my head, everything blurred except the little
space around Charles and his outstretched hand. I
was moving towards it, as if in a dream, as if I was
sliding towards him on rollers. I couldn't see Annie.
A triumphant smile was breaking out across his
face. But before I could take his hand, there was a
loud bang from behind him and the fogginess had
gone. Annie was hunched on the floor, massaging
her throat and gasping. Charles, focussed so intently
on me had let his grip on Annie's neck slacken and
she'd managed to break free. He hissed and turned
around. His face, that only a moment ago had looked
so paternal and caring, had transformed into a
snarling horror of a face, teeth bared. I started back
and staggered as my legs refused to support me.

"The candle! Get the candle!" Annie had recovered
and jumped onto Charles' back, unbalancing him
and knocking them both into the piles of treasure.
Her words clicked. I leapt for the table, towards the

machine. There was only a small disk of wax left in the candle holder. Was it enough? I struck the match and a small flame flickered up the wood. But I couldn't get the candle to light. The wick was not nearly long enough.

"Hurry!" shouted Annie. There was a terrific banging and crashing as they fought among the pile of treasure, hissing and snarling. I ripped a section of my shirt off and stuffed it inside. When the flame did catch it caught far too quickly, and the dry material was almost gone before I could react. The light flowed through the mirror, a pearly white, but it was directed in the opposite direction to Charles and when I tried to move it, it was jammed.

"Annie, it's jammed! I can't move it!"

"You stupid child!" sneered Charles. "Did you really think I would make it so easy?"

He had jammed it! He'd known what we were attempting, always one step ahead of us. I locked eyes with Annie but instead of seeing the fear I felt in them, there was a calculating expression. Then I saw a little smile form on her face.

"No," she whispered. "And that is what makes it so predictable." She moved so quickly I missed it. Her feet connected with Charles' abdomen and he flew back, towards the white light. The minute he touched it I felt a trembling under my feet as the table started shaking violently. I was afraid for a moment it would break. Annie was beside me in an instant. I opened my mouth to ask but she shook her head.

"Watch."

I watched. Charles hung suspended in the air, trapped in the white light as if it was solid. His form kept changing, moving between the man I could see now, and a skeleton much like the one I had seen Annie turn into. The table was shaking and shaking and Annie pulled us both back against the wall, bracing her hand there. The borders of the light started to move, dividing themselves into long snake-light tubes. They writhed around Charles' form. The edge of his body started breaking away. A high-pitched squealing came from the machine, accompanied by a large clicking and ticking, like a clock.

"His time is catching up on him," Annie whispered in my ear.

"No one can be timeless forever." The light surrounding him grew brighter and brighter, until it was almost as bright as lightning. Annie turned her eyes away and pushed me down as well. The squealing heightened in dynamic and pitch and I squinted against the ringing in my ears. I covered them with my hands but it made no difference. I could feel Annie's head pressing into my right shoulder and water from her wet hair running down my neck. The wall dug into my left shoulder. Just before I was sure my ears would burst there was an enormous bang and a wind so strong that it swept my hair out of its ponytail. A howling joined the squealing; I clenched my teeth against the pain, a howling so loud and intense that my bones hurt with the noise of it. It was more powerful than any thunder I'd ever heard. I clung to the wall and peeked at Charles. His body was surrounded by a fine red mist and I covered my eyes again, disgusted. Then, as suddenly as it had started, it stopped. I looked at the machine. All that remained of Charles was a fine dust, drifting through the air.

"Is he gone?" I asked, walking forward. Annie

stopped me.

"Let me go," she advised. She approached the spot carefully. The wax had completely gone from the candle and there was no trace of my shirt. Annie bent down and touched the dust. Then she looked up at me. "He's gone."

"So, are they all gone?" She didn't answer. Her head shot up suddenly as if she was thinking about something. "Bella." And she tore out of the door, leaving me there.

§

I followed, but slower. Apparently she wanted to be alone. Bella was where we'd left her, lying in the corner, spread-eagled on the wooden floor. Annie was crouched over her. I looked around but the boy, Zac, was nowhere to be seen

"Bella?" I stood in the doorway, feeling very awkward and intrusive. Bella's head was moving feebly.

"She's waking up," Annie said, helping her to sit up.

"Why didn't she go with the others?"

"She was the sacrifice that enabled everyone else to be the way they were. She survived the light, and she saved me. Therefore, she was never really tied to Charles and her life had nothing to do with his." I nodded in understanding.

"Ann?" Bella's voice was young and sweet, so different from the sneering rasp. Her face looked confused as she struggled up, holding onto her sister's arm. Her eyes roved the walls carefully. "Where are we Ann?"

"Still in the Hall. But he's gone now. You are free and so am I." Bella gave a little gasp as if she was in pain.

"Oh Ann, I am so sorry. You know I never meant to

hurt you. I never meant any of the things I said to you." But Annie was shaking her head, smiling. "Don't worry about that now. I'm sorry too." Bella's brow creased with puzzlement. "For what?"

"For bringing you to this place." I turned away as Annie's voice cracked and tears spilled down her cheeks. It wasn't my place to be here. I shouldn't be looking at this. This was private.

"I never should have. We should have stayed where we were. We could have died back there, with our family, not here. Do you forgive me?" Bella smiled. "Of course. But you must forgive Lizzie and everyone else you've hated here. I'm better now and you've hated her for long enough. Even when we were in the chest, she still felt sorry. She has only ever wanted to be your friend."

"I didn't hate her. I hated what she did."

"But even so, that's over now. Forgive her as well."

"I forgive her for you." And the black head fell down onto the little brown one and stayed there. I went to step outside but I didn't miss the next words. "Be free. Go, and be free."

I stepped back inside. Bella's body was slowly crumbling, not in the harsh way that Charles' had but softly, gently. Her face adopted a look of perfect tranquillity and when I blinked against the film of tears that had covered my vision, there was only a pile of clothing left, covered in a fine pink dust. When I looked again, Annie was gone as well and I was alone.

§

I knew where Annie would be now. I was right. She was kneeling on the ground in the valley. I ran down the slope to stand beside her.

"Annie? Are you okay?"

"Oh yes," she smiled. "I'm fine." She looked up at me. "And if I'm not fine, I'll get better, won't I?" She gave me another smile which I half-heartedly returned.

"What's the matter, Rose?"

"I don't get it," I replied slowly. "You seem so happy but you just lost your sister all over again." Annie didn't answer right away. "But that's where they are meant to be. Charles as well. And everyone else. They all died hundreds of years ago; that's their proper place."

"But your sister ..."

"Is happier where she is now," broke in Annie, stretching her legs out on the grass. She patted the ground beside her and I shuffled up closer to her, still confused.

"Yes. She's much happier. And now it's all finished. It's done." I pulled my knees up to my chest and rested my chin on them. "So what will you do now?" Annie gave another secretive smile. "I have one last thing to do, I think, before I decide that." And she jumped to her feet, holding out a hand to pull me up. We returned to the house. It was very quiet there now. I gave a fleeting look at the crumpled banister and broken doors and sighed. When Mum and Dad came back, I'd have some explaining to do. Annie followed my gaze but said nothing. I followed her to my room. The wall was still in pieces on the floor and dust had settled over everything. Annie picked her way through the sea of wreckage on the carpet and approached the door. She took the key from around her neck and held it out to me.

"Here. You have it. I don't need all those things anymore."

I looked at the key, dangling on its ribbon and shook my head. "I can't Annie. That's too much to give a person."

"I thought you would say that," Annie muttered. "Take it. I'm giving it to you. You deserve it, besides," her mouth curling up into a mischievous smile, "how are you going to pacify your parents unless you give them something they can fix the house with?" I returned a tense smile and took the key, tucking it away into my pocket. Annie turned to face the door for a moment and put her hand on the handle, as if she wanted to open it and then stepped away, twisting around to face me again.

"Oh, yes, and I need to give you this," and reaching into her other pocket she took out another key. I recognized it immediately.

"The key for the attics! Where did you find it?"

"Lying on the floor. I think you need it back." I took it and pocketed it as well. Annie gave the room one last look and rubbed her hands together.

"Well, that's done now. Do you want to go to the valley again? And then I should go before your parents get back." I had no preference and so together we returned to the valley. We sat in silence side by side, right next to the letters, still laid out in the valley. Annie had closed her eyes but she opened them when she felt my gaze on her and pointed toward the woods.

"In there is where Zac's tribe lived. They're all dead now of course." She moved her hand to the right slightly. "And that's where I first saw Zac on his horse, coming out of the woods." I nodded. She looked at me.

"I heard what Charles said to you. You mustn't think about it. He was lying." I nodded, looking away to hide my tears. It was stupid to have thought he could repair my family, give me the parents I wanted.

"Your parents do think highly of you, you know."

I swallowed. "I know. But I wish they would show it, just a little bit more." She nodded. I didn't want words of pity and I didn't get them. I rubbed the tears away from my eyes and posed my own question.

"Annie, where will you go?" She stopped, interlinked her fingers, and took a deep breath.

"I thought we'd come to this. Now that everyone is really dead it means that the curse, if that is what you want to call it, really is broken. Which means," and she took another deep breath as if she herself couldn't believe it, "I'm free as well."

"How do you know?" In reply, she showed me her hand. Tracing her palm was a thin shallow cut. A scab covered it but it wasn't healing.

"Usually my wounds heal immediately." I looked at the gash she had had on her forehead and sure enough, it was gone.

"So how are you still alive?" My questions sounded flat as if I was refusing to believe. In reality, I couldn't get my mind around the fact she wasn't cursed and the consequences of that.

"Because I still want to be. I have a little time left to stay alive before my many years catch up on me. Like Bella, my life didn't depend on Charles's. I became like this because of my choices. Therefore it is my choice as to when I die," and she smiled as she said it. I struggled to process this.

"So, you'll die?" I asked, my voice sounding thin and weak. Annie tilted her head to one side and twisted her fingers in her lap.

"Yes, I will. But I've waited a long time for it Rose,

and it should have happened many, many years ago." She'd stood up so I stood up too, blinking in confusion. Was she just going to die? Just like that? "So, I'll say goodbye now, I think."

Before my eyes she began to change. Her hair twisted itself up into a tight bun and her dress rippled once and transformed into a long grey one, fraying at the bottom. The sleeves came right down to her wrists and at the end were a few holes, as if moths had attacked it. An apron that looked like it used to be white but now had greyed slightly was tied around her waist and her hands looked rough and calloused. She didn't look like the Annie I knew; she looked younger or maybe older, as if she didn't belong here, standing next to me. A timeless frame of the girl I had known. A being trapped through the ages and now free. Annie gasped suddenly and exclaimed, "Oh, yes, I almost forgot. I want you to have this," and she slid something off her wrist. I took it, curiously. It was a braid, made of strands of plaited hair. There were five colours woven into it: two blacks, a blond, a chestnut brown and a reddish brown.

"This one was mine. I put Zac on mine as well and you are there too." I slid it onto my wrist.

"Thanks, Annie."

"Ann," she replied. "My name is Ann."

The people behind her wavered into sight, three of them, two girls and a boy. They appeared out of thin air, standing quietly behind her. When Ann saw them, she didn't seem surprised. On the other hand, her face lit up with a blissful beam and she exclaimed joyfully, "Bella!" Her sister pushed herself forward. She looked so much younger now, maybe only seven or eight.

"Are you coming at last?" I could see right through her but her form was still defined, pulsating slightly. But when she took Ann's hand, her hand became solid and I could see Ann holding it tightly as if she was never going to let it go ever again. Bella smiled and said, "All our family is waiting for you. They missed you as well, you know." Ann nodded, her face overwhelmed with happiness. I saw the boy come forward as well, the one I had last seen with a snarl on his face, pinned against the wall. He took Ann's other hand.

"Will you do as you are told this time?" He grinned. I didn't understand what he was talking about but Ann did and she laughed, ruffling his hair.

"Yes, I'm coming now."

There was a taller girl as well standing there, smiling at Ann. Her hair was the same blond as on my braid. "Lizzie, I'm sorry," Ann said and the girl nodded but didn't say a word, only smiled even more.

"I'm coming now," Ann repeated. I lowered my head to blink away the tears that had sprung to my eyes so didn't see Ann run towards me. She flung her arms around me and I hugged her back, feeling the tears run now, however much I tried to hold them in. I heard her whisper shakily next to my ear as if she was laughing or crying as well, "Goodbye Rose. Don't ever forget me, okay?"

"I don't think I'd be able to," I rejoined. Annie let me go and smiled. Then, without another word, she returned to Bella and took her hand. They started to walk away, all of them. Across the valley they went and as they walked, they rose higher and higher, still walking, their clothes flapping around their ankles as they went.

"Goodbye Ann," I whispered. I went back to the house.

The End

About me

I am 14 years old and currently at Croydon High
School. I have been writing for eight years but
Timeless is my first published book, taking me two
years to complete; I have always wanted to be a
published author. I love creating worlds of my own
in my head. English Literature and History are my
favourite subjects at school. An avid reader I also
enjoy long distance running; I get a lot of inspiration
for my writing while running. Fantasy adventure
and paranormal are my favourite genres; I find them
really interesting.